S0-BYA-560

FOUR HORSES FOR TISHTRY

OTHER BOOKS BY CHELSEA QUINN YARBRO

Dead and Buried
False Dawn
Messages from Michael

The Saint-Germain Cycle:
Hotel Transylvania
The Palace
Blood Games
Path of the Eclipse
Tempting Fate

And for Young Adults
Locadio's Apprentice

FOUR HORSES FOR TISHTRY

CHELSEA QUINN YARBRO

HARPER & ROW, PUBLISHERS

Four Horses for Tishtry
Copyright © 1985 by Chelsea Quinn Yarbro
All rights reserved. No part of this book may be
used or reproduced in any manner whatsoever without
written permission except in the case of brief quotations
embodied in critical articles and reviews. Printed in
the United States of America. For information address
Harper & Row Junior Books, 10 East 53rd Street,
New York, N.Y. 10022. Published simultaneously in
Canada by Fitzhenry & Whiteside Limited, Toronto.
Designed by Joyce Hopkins
1 2 3 4 5 6 7 8 9 10
First Edition

Library of Congress Cataloging in Publication Data
Yarbro, Chelsea Quinn, 1942–
    Four horses for Tishtry.

    Summary: Tishtry's wish to buy her family's freedom
from slavery in the Roman Empire inspires her to
perform dangerous feats of stunt riding.
    [1. Slavery—Rome—Fiction.   2. Rome—Fiction.
3. Trick riding—Fiction]   I. Title.
PZ7.Y1954Fo   1985   [Fic]   84-48341
ISBN 0-06-026638-4
ISBN 0-06-026639-2 (lib. bdg.)

for
KAY
since it isn't romantic enough
for George

CHAPTER

I

As the big dapple mare came out of the turn at a gallop, the girl crouched on her back, braced her feet, and carefully straightened up, her knees flexed to absorb the mare's pace. Together they flashed around the practice arena, once, twice, three times, the mare galloping steadily, the girl standing on her rump, arms raised.

"Better!" shouted the girl's father, who had been watching critically. "Much better!"

Tishtry knew it was folly to try to answer him—for one thing, she would not be heard, for another, she might startle her mount, and that would be too risky. She waved her fists instead, and waited for the right moment to dismount. She leaned with the horse through the turn, then shifted her weight so that she could spring free. With a whoop, she vaulted into the air, did a somersault, and landed on her feet, arms still raised.

The mare continued on down the length of the arena,

slowing to a trot now that she was riderless.

"That was more like it," Tishtry's father said gruffly, though his smile told more than the tone of his voice. He whistled through his teeth for the mare, then gave his attention to his daughter once more. "What do you think of it?"

"Well," she answered carefully, "I did *not* get up as easily as I wanted to, and I wasn't as well balanced on the first turn as I should have been, but most of it was pretty good. The last circuit was the best, and the dismount was almost perfect."

Soduz nodded. "That's a good evaluation. I'd have to say that you might try to turn a little more to the side once you're standing up: the people in the stands want to see your face."

"*I* want to see where my horse is going," Tishtry countered. "You've always told me that should come first."

"Well, and so it should," Soduz said as if there were no contradiction in his two statements.

"But if I'm supposed to watch where the horse is going, how can I look toward the stands?" Tishtry braced her hands on her hips, trying to keep from laughing, which would annoy her father more than he would ever admit to her.

"It's a matter of circumstances," Soduz told her, looking a trifle stiff, as she had known he would. He was not a large man, but he was taller than she, rangy of build but with a barrel chest that gave him enormous strength and a large, resonant voice that seemed much bigger than he was. He regarded his daughter with a degree of pride. "You have to consider what's best to

2

do. You've been riding since you were three. Remember that when you are in the arena, you are there to entertain as much as to ride, and you must decide where to put your greatest concentration."

Tishtry grinned. "If you tell me so, Father, then I believe you." She was dressed very much as he was, in knee-length leather breeches and a short, sleeveless, close-fitting leather tunica. Her belt was made of alternate links of brass and bone, which were to bring her courage and luck. On her feet she wore very soft boots of reverse leather, so that the rough surface of the soles would help her grip her horse's back when she rode standing.

"And you're teasing me, girl, which isn't right." He put his wide hand on her shoulder. "You're going out on your own soon, Tishtry, and I'm not going to be with you to remind you of all these things. I've trained you as best I know how, but you will have to learn to judge for yourself. Never forget that we are Armenians, for all our master lives in Cappadocia, and we have our honor to uphold; while we still have time, ask the things you need to know to do this."

"But what are they?" Tishtry asked, trying to be sensible. "I've learned everything you've taught me, you admit that yourself. It's true enough that I can do it all here, in this little arena, but when I'm before a crowd, with the sun beating down on me and the noise, it may be that I'll have to learn other things, things you don't know and I can't guess yet." She reached out to pat the neck of the mare, who had ambled up to them. "Look at her. Nine years old and she goes like a champion. Nothing ever bothers her."

"Rezicha is a good horse," her father agreed, giving the mare an offhanded pat. "You two work well together."

"I know," Tishtry said, not quite able to hide her sigh. "I'll miss her."

Soduz gave her a bracing smile, meant to encourage her. "Come now, girl, it isn't for several months yet. You have much to do before you'll be on your way. And with our master, who knows how many times he'll change his mind between now and the time you leave?" He started toward the fence, his daughter and the mare coming after him. "You will need to take a little time to make yourself ready. Barantosz says that now you're almost thirteen, he wants to see you establish yourself, and that means the arena."

At the mention of their owner, Tishtry giggled. "I can hear him. And I'll bet he was fussing with the hems of his tunicae when he said it."

"No; with the ends of his sash," Soduz corrected her, laughing a bit in spite of himself. "You know as well as I do how he fusses. He'll have to see progress from you."

"But I *have* progressed," Tishtry protested. "You've told me so yourself."

"And you, I trust, are aware of it as well." He grabbed the top rail of the fence and swung up onto it, signaling to Tishtry to do the same.

"I hope I am," she said slowly as she climbed. "I'm not sure."

"Stop it," Soduz chided her. "If you're not sure . . . You can't afford to be hesitant, girl. We bestiarii have to

4

know every moment how well we do, or our lives are at risk."

"They're at risk in any case. When Janoun was my age, he . . ." She could not finish.

"Your brother was a good boy," Soduz said in a strange voice. "But a reckless one; he didn't remember the limits, and he forgot his horses. Those of us who perform with horses must not forget them. We're not like charioteers, who simply race around the arena; we're bestiarii, and our animals are as much a part of our performance as we are—*more* than we are, often."

As if to agree, Rezicha nudged at Soduz's leg with her nose, whickering softly.

"Yes, girl," Soduz crooned, reaching out to rub the mare's ears. "Good girl. You're a pride, aren't you?"

Tishtry grinned. "How could you have forgot Rezicha?"

"Now listen, Tishtry," her father said. "You've taken on a lot. You are going to try to do what none of the rest of us have: perform in the largest arenae and gain enough wealth to free all of us. Don't let that overwhelm you." He paused. "Janoun couldn't have done it. You have a chance to do this."

She drew a deep breath, feeling both proud and frightened at this reminder. It was a great honor to be the one the family had such hopes for, but what if she failed. "I'll do everything I can," she promised her father.

"Fine," he murmured, then looked at her squarely. "That does not mean you're to let yourself be abused or endangered. I've lost one child to stupidity already, and I am not prepared to lose another. An arena slave

5

who cannot perform with skill has no value to anyone."
He stared away toward the distant outline of the mountains. "A dead one is nothing."

"Yes, my father," Tishtry said quietly, thinking of her brother.

A short while later, Soduz spoke to her again. "You're the best of the family, girl, and you are the one who can do the most. You're young enough that you have at least a dozen years to work in the arena before it becomes too dangerous, and you have sense enough to be able to train others when you are done with performing. That gives you great worth. If you're fortunate in your masters, the day will come when not one of us will have to wear a collar."

"If I can save the money, you will all be free," she vowed to him, and felt a glow of pride within her once more. She would do it!

"I know that, Tishtry." He gave her single long braid an affectionate tug. "Just do not be tempted to recklessness. Not even freedom is worth the loss of you." He patted the mare's neck as he spoke. "We have been slaves for longer than my grandfather could remember, and we have done well enough for ourselves. If we sold all our horses, we could be free—true enough—but then what would we do?" His musing ended abruptly as he caught sight of one of the other bestiarii on the far side of the practice arena. "Gontho! What are you bringing in here?"

The squat Persian looked up from the cage he was handling. "A new bear, half grown! You'd better get your horse out of here, Soduz!"

"Gods of the air and fishes!" Soduz swore as he

6

scrambled down off the fence, taking Rezicha by the mane and leading her to one of the gates in the wall. "Tishtry, go see if the training ring is free. You can work the yearlings for the rest of the afternoon."

Tishtry did as she was told, but her mind was not on the rambunctious colts that cavorted and scampered on the end of the lunge; it was on the future and her debut in the Great Games. The Ludi Maximi! She had heard those words since she had been old enough to speak, and they had become magic to her. The heroes of the Games were famous throughout the Empire. There were times she hoped that she would be one of the heroes, famed from Gaul to Africa, with her own retinue and followers. It was what any bestiarii would want. She imagined herself, crowned with laurel, riding in a chariot garlanded in flowers while more people than there were in the world shouted and clapped for her.

The colts bucked, and one reached out to nip the other. Tishtry came back to herself at once. It would not do to let her mind drift that way. If she let herself be caught up in impossible wishes, she would end up leaving the arena through the Gates of Death. "Better to do your work," she told herself sternly. These fancies of hers could wait for the time when she had proved herself.

On her thirteenth birthday, Tishtry was given a special meal and a number of gifts to mark her leaving childhood. To honor the event, her master joined her family for the celebration, turning the occasion into a formal one.

"It has been exciting to watch you," her master said

7

as he sat with the rest of them in the grape arbor at the back of his villa. "You are a most promising young woman."

This was the first time anyone had called Tishtry a young woman, and for a moment it worried her; now she was thirteen, her master could give her to one of his other slaves to have children. She had been assured that he would not, but a man like Barantosz often changed his mind. She took care to speak respectfully. "It is my hope that I will be able to demonstrate myself worthy of your trust."

Chimbue Barantosz was of mixed Armenian and Persian heritage, shaped like a wine cask and with a long, sagging hound's face. He was habitually cold and wore two to three woolen tunicae all the time, with Persian leggings to give him added warmth. His favorite color was red. "Yes, yes. I'm counting on that, of course. We all are. Your father has made his plans clear to me. I approve; do not doubt that. But to earn enough to free him and his two wives and your brother and sisters, that will take real ability, Tishtry." He wagged fat, stubby fingers at her, attempting to look severe and instead reminding everyone of an overgrown infant. "I'll do what I can to give you every opportunity, but you cannot expect me to advance you beyond your skills. Can you?"

"It would be wrong of her," Soduz said, stepping into the awkward moment. "And none of us would want it."

"I am determined to do my best to excel," Tishtry told her master, trying to find the best phrases to gain his support.

"A good thing. You have every reason to make the effort, that much is clear." He chuckled and the others dutifully laughed. "Not that there haven't been other offers. Not a week ago, Pilanis Shemic came to me with a generous offer—"

"What!" Soduz burst out. "And you said nothing?"

"I said no," Barantosz said, looking hurt. "I am not one to go back on my word, even when it is given to a slave. I told you two years ago, Soduz, that your daughter would have her chance, and I will see that she has it." He paused. "I know that it is not the same as it was with Janoun, but when your son died, I felt the loss as well."

There was silence in the arbor, as intense as it was brief. "Yes, but that is in the past," Soduz said as if there had been no silence at all. "And now it is time for my daughter to make her attempt. I know she is able to do the thing. Give her the chariot and the horses, and in three years, she will be in Roma, in the Circus Maximus itself, and the whole populace will cry her name in praise!"

The others echoed his cheer, but Tishtry remained thoughtful. "I think that it may take more than three years. We are in Cappadocia, and it is a long way to Roma. I have heard it said that they are more demanding there, because of the grandness of the place and because they see everything from everywhere all the time."

"That's what they boast of, at any case," Tishtry's older sister said with a toss of her head. "Anyone who performs well would be welcome there, I think. And we know that Tishtry performs well."

9

"Macon is right," Soduz said emphatically. "Yes, they will want to see her because she is as good as any of them."

"I hope," Tishtry said very quietly. "I will do everything I can, so that all of you will be proud."

Macon reached over and touched her arm. "You're the bravest of all of us. You don't mind the crowds and the shouting and the rush of it. I think I would go mad if I had to live that way."

Tishtry shrugged. "It's part of it, that's all. In time you get used to it." She could not bring herself to admit that she did not like the constant rush and pressure of the circus, and what little exposure she had had to it terrified her. The thought of appearing in the Circus Maximus before all the people of Roma made her feel faintly sick. She had never performed for more than a hundred spectators, yet she knew that thousands came to the great amphitheaters; thousands scared her.

"She will be a credit to all of us," Barantosz said, raising his wine cup and drinking to Tishtry. "You will do very well, Tishtry. All of us are certain of it."

"How wonderful," Tishtry said dutifully, a sinking sensation in her middle as she spoke. How could she ever live up to the hopes of her family, she wondered. What would she do if she failed? The thought haunted her all through the meal, and by sunset she felt she carried all of them on her shoulders.

Macon held out the supple leather she had been working, holding it up to the muted light so that Tishtry could see its luster. "For the bridles. I haven't found the right leather yet for your reins, but I will."

Tishtry nodded. "I know. You always know what will work best." She pulled up a stool and watched while Macon continued her task. "How long will it take to finish, do you think?"

"It will depend on how soon Barantosz can get the brass fittings I requested. If he wants the buckles and eyes to last, I'll have to use brass instead of horn. The horn is flexible, but for what you'll be doing, you will require sturdier tack." She took out an awl and began to punch holes in the leather. "For the saddle, I have asked for the leather from Hind. It is tougher and you'll find that once I fix the horn, you will be able to ride without slipping."

"And the girths?" Tishtry asked, thinking of the last time she had slipped because the girth had come loose.

"The same leather as the saddle, and more brass fittings. That should make a difference, don't you think?" Macon took a long, thin strip of leather and began to bind the punched leather. "This will make it stronger without making it less flexible. That ought to be some help. That's the trouble with you going away—I won't be able to do your repairs for you when you need them."

"Then perhaps you should come with me, Macon, at least for a while, until we're sure the tack is all right." Tishtry tried not to sound too eager so that her sister would not realize how much she dreaded being completely alone and away from anyone she knew. It was exciting to think of the opportunities that might come her way, but the loneliness frightened her, although she had yet to experience it.

"I'll ask our father. He's the one to speak to Barantosz, no matter what's decided." Macon gave a little

11

sigh. "I hope I'll be able to go. I'd like to have more time with you, and it would be good to travel. And if I don't go with you now, when will I ever, unless our master has to sell us for debts sometime."

"Is that likely?" Tishtry asked, suddenly worried that even if she earned enough money, she would not have enough to find her family and buy their freedom. Barantosz had agreed on his prices, but another master might not be willing to keep the price low, and Tishtry had heard that petitioning a magistrate to set a fair price could take more than a year.

"Oh, I don't think so," Macon said with the sophistication of her sixteen years. "He claims that he gambles too much, but he has never lost so much as a horse for it, let alone a slave." She looked toward the window. "I have another hour of light before I'll need lamps. Let me get on with this, Tishtry. We'll talk after we eat."

The two girls had different mothers, and for that reason did not look very much alike. Both were olive skinned and dark haired, but Tishtry was small, big boned and well muscled, with a wide, strong face. Macon was taller, softer, with quick, clever hands and a gentle smile that played about the corners of her generous mouth when she spoke, turning her ordinary features pretty. As they stood side by side in the tack room, their differences were more marked than their similarities. Their voices sounded alike, although Tishtry spoke more energetically than her older sister did.

"I'll have a word with the grooms," Tishtry said as she went toward the door. "There's so much to do, and I'm . . . worried I might forget something, or leave

12

something behind. What do I need, leaving home?"

"Don't be in too much of a rush," Macon replied. "You have time enough to check your requirements. You need not leave us for a month or so."

"Or more," Tishtry said, frowning as she went out into the bright afternoon.

CHAPTER

II

All four of the horses were two years old. Tishtry had worked them for Soduz for half a year, and had liked them. She watched them as they were yoked up to the special chariot she used.

"What do you think of them now?" Soduz asked as one of the grooms led them across the practice arena toward father and daughter.

"I think that Dozei is yoked up too tightly," Tishtry answered. "He's nervous, and if you press him, he only becomes worse."

"Then you adjust it," Soduz told her, and stood, his hands braced on his hips, while Tishtry went to the groom and started to adjust the yoke. "What do you think of them as a team?"

"Nicely balanced," Tishtry answered, not raising her voice much. "Shirdas will need special work if he's going to be on the inside. He's not quite strong enough yet, but with some extra time on the lunge, he ought to be all right." She patted the chestnut, automatically checking the bit in his mouth. "Look at his chin. He's going to have a square nose when he's fully grown."

"Does he strike you as being a little short in the back?" Soduz inquired as he came toward Tishtry. "That could mean trouble later on."

"Oh, I don't think it's a problem. Look at his legs. His stance is good." Her voice had softened. "You're a good boy, aren't you, Shirdas?"

As if in response to this, Shirdas wagged his head vehemently, snorting.

"Well, so much for agreement." Soduz laughed. "What about Immit? They say pale horses are bad luck."

"How could Immit be bad luck?" Tishtry smiled as she patted the silver-dun horse. "Look at the barrel on her. Look at her neck. And she shines so nicely. She's a perfect horse."

Immit gave a low whinny, and Tishtry blew into her nostrils when the mare dropped her nose onto the girl's shoulder.

"Dozei is a better color," Soduz remarked, giving the sorrel a pat. "He is colored for courage. And the blaze on his face is a good omen."

"Immit is fine," Tishtry insisted. "And so is Amath; bays are known to be steady," she added to defend the four of them.

"But you know that a team should be matched. That's the usual way. A mismatched team like this one will cause some laughs in the arena," Soduz pointed out.

15

"To have such a mixed lot . . . well, there are those who believe that horses of diverse colors can never be made into a true team."

"Anyone who'd say such a thing is a fool. It doesn't matter if the coats match, but that the strides and paces match. The rest is unimportant. In fact," Tishtry said, concentrating on the horses, "I like the variety of them. If they were all dun or sorrel or chestnut, they would not be distinctive. They are unalike, and that reminds me that they are not the same horse copied over and over. If they were too much alike, I might confuse them in the arena, and that might be dangerous. This way, I can't forget how different each of my horses is, and that I must treat them differently."

"There's some sense in that," Soduz allowed. "Our master won't understand, but I'll try to explain it so he will not think you mock him."

"Why should my preference for these horses mock him?" she asked without paying much attention.

"Are you certain you would not like others better?" Soduz inquired.

"Better for what?" Tishtry asked, becoming impatient with her father. "For show? Or is my judgment of horseflesh in question?"

"Only in terms of what you want. Our master has said—and it shows, he *can* do the proper thing every now and then—that you are to be given four two-year-olds for your team, and if you are fond of these, then—" He was not able to finish. With a squeal of delight, Tishtry threw herself into her father's arms, for once paying little attention to the alarm she gave her horses.

"There, girl. There, that's enough," Soduz protested

16

as Tishtry tried to hug him and jump up and down at the same time.

"Mine? *Really?* Are they mine?" she demanded when she could speak again. "Truly?"

"Barantosz gave the authorization yesterday, and I took the most likely four in the stables. You've been working with these brutes for over a year, you know them and they go well together. So your master wants you to have them for your own."

"Completely?" Her face fell when she wondered if Barantosz intended to deed them to her, or merely let her have them for her performing.

"As your own, of course," Soduz said at once. "He is aware that to do less would reflect badly on his reputation. You will have to train your team to do tricks. That would be the case, no matter what horses you choose. If you're satisfied with these four, then I'll enter their names and descriptions with the head groom and the documents will be sent to the magistrates."

At last Tishtry believed him. "Will I have a copy of it?"

"But you can't read," her father said, laughing kindly.

"I might need it, you know. There might be doubts, and the protests of a slave without proof don't get much attention."

What she said was true enough, but Soduz reminded her, "If they're your property, they can't be seized, and if their ownership is in doubt, a magistrate must be brought to decide the matter. Barantosz told you this before."

"It wasn't the same. And I was afraid he might change his mind."

Soduz gave in. "All right. I'll ask the scribe to make a copy for you to take with you. But don't forget that more than half the bestiarii who work with horses own their teams. You remember that Scythian who came here with a team of bears? Well, those were his, and no one was inclined to dispute it."

"That's different," Tishtry said slowly. "No one wants to ride bears or hitch a pair of them to a biga. A good horse is another matter, and these are very good horses, all four of them." She still found it hard to think of the horses as her own, and she touched Immit's glossy neck to reassure herself.

"You have a point," Soduz conceded. "And one that Barantosz should understand. It might be a good precaution, once you're away from here. Some of the Masters of Bestiarii are overeager to make use of good teams. With your deed, there could be no question of misuse. I wouldn't want you to have to enter the arena with your horses against lions and tigers."

"Do they *do* that?" Tishtry was shocked, for although she knew a fair amount about the Great Games, she had only seen the smallest and mildest of spectacles when the local horse breeders got together for informal races at the time of wine pressing in the autumn. "Do they send horses against lions?"

"Yes, they do, and worse besides. Don't worry," he went on, seeing how troubled she was. "Barantosz will give specific instructions that you're to be exempt from such presentation. The training of your team should be argument enough, but you never know. Some ambitious sponsor of the Games might think that because he is editor, he has the right to demand 'something a little different.' ''

"Can editoris do that?" Tishtry asked.

"Depends on how much money they're willing to spend on their Games, and how high their rank is. If a Senator decided that he wanted such display and he had gold enough to afford it, it's not impossible. When an editor sponsors Games, it's his right to choose the entertainment."

Tishtry's deep misgivings increased as she heard this. "Father," she said quietly, "what happens if I refuse to do what an editor wants? Would that keep me out of the Games, or would there be punishment because I'm an arena slave and a bestiarii?"

"If Barantosz permits an editor such use of you and your team, then you can't refuse without getting into trouble." Soduz knew she was not satisfied with that explanation. "But the editor must ask, since you don't usually work with wild animals, and I doubt that Barantosz would endanger his investment in you, to say nothing of your horses, by permitting you to be exposed to any greater danger than the tricks you do."

"Is there any way he can say that, so there won't be an argument about it?" Tishtry asked, still not pleased.

"Naturally. And a man of his cautious nature is probably prepared to make such a statement. Look, girl, Barantosz raises horses and mules for the Legions, and that makes him an important man to the Romans. Cappadocia is valuable to them, and you may be sure that no Roman is going to offend an Armenian horse breeder over one slave. It isn't worth it."

Tishtry was not entirely convinced, but she did not press her father. "I'd better finish exercising . . . *my* team."

"*Your* team," he agreed. "And I trust you'll never regret your choices."

"How could I?" she called after him as he left her alone with her racing chariot and four horses, which were her only possessions other than her tack and clothes. She looked at her team and grinned. "*I* don't think you're mismatched," she told the horses. "I think you're perfect."

For two weeks, Tishtry spent the greater part of every day working her team. She took them out on the practice trails, worked them individually and in combination, ran them through their paces on the lunge, rode them as well as yoked them up to her chariot, and spent hours in the practice ring getting them used to working together. Every sign of improvement made her glow with pride; every mistake seemed almost a personal insult.

"I think they're almost ready to start learning the tricks," Tishtry confided to her sister Macon as they sat alone in their little bedroom late one evening.

"The saddles aren't finished yet. I've got bridles for three of them." Macon was not easily excited, and now her unflustered attitude annoyed Tishtry.

"Don't you want to come and watch?"

Macon shrugged. "Why should I? I've seen your tricks many times. And if it turns out that I'm to go with you when you leave, I'll see them often then. Right now I'd rather spend the time with the saddles. Now that I know which horses they're for, I can make a perfect fit on each." She smiled, showing her pride in her work.

Tishtry tossed her head. "Don't you even *care* about my tricks?"

"Well, of course I do," Macon answered, as if unaware of Tishtry's irritation.

"It doesn't sound like it," Tishtry snapped, her face flushing.

"Tishtry," Macon said very seriously, "I saw Janoun get killed. I could only stare while it happened. You weren't there. You don't know what it was like, watching our brother dragged and trampled. I don't *like* watching trick riders and trick charioteers anymore. I can't get the memory of Janoun out of my mind while I watch. And though I know you're a better rider than he, I can't help but be afraid."

"Oh," Tishtry said quietly. It had never occurred to her that Macon might be worried for her, and the discovery of this startled her, making her feel troubled and shamed that she had not realized it before.

"In time I may change. But for now, Tishtry, don't ask me to watch you any more than I must." She turned away before Tishtry could say anything more, and she did not speak again until she was ready for sleep, when she looked at her younger sister. "You *are* better than Janoun. That's something."

With that thought for consolation, Tishtry fell into a restless sleep that was haunted by dreams of strange places and unexpected accidents.

Chimbue Barantosz toddled over to Tishtry as she came out of the practice arena. "I am pleased with what you are doing, girl," he announced loudly. He did not

21

look pleased; his face was set in a perpetual frown, and when he spoke, he did not meet her eyes, but stared over her shoulder at some distant point. He was fiddling with the ends of his sash.

"That is gratifying," Tishtry said in her most respectful manner as she gathered the traces in her hands. "I must walk my team, Master. They're sweaty and it will hurt them if they're allowed to stand this way."

"Of course, of course," he said at once, and fell into step beside her while she led her team toward the stable yard. "I have been speaking to your father about you. We must make plans, you know."

There was nothing that Tishtry could correctly say in response, so she remained quiet. She let herself and her team into the cooling area and began the familiar routine of leading her horses while they cooled. It surprised her to find Barantosz keeping step with her.

"You will be pleased to know that I have registered your ownership of your team, and there will be another copy of the deed for you. That was a wise request. I told Soduz that he has a clever daughter; it is true."

"Thank you, Master," Tishtry said, trying to puzzle out what Barantosz could want of her.

"And I hear you are improving daily. That is commendable." He cleared his throat. "There will be Games in Apollonia in April. That is five months away. Are you prepared to be ready to perform there?"

The question came so abruptly that Tishtry stopped walking and was bumped into by Dozei. She resumed walking, a bit embarrassed at being inept with her horses. "Five months? Why not? I will have these horses ready before then."

"I will arrange for a party of local horse breeders and wine growers to watch you before then. You will see how they like you, and listen to what they have to say, so that you can correct any faults they may notice. You're very young, girl, and you still have much to learn." His face was a bit flushed, but whether from awkwardness or from exercise, Tishtry did not know. "I expect you to do very well."

"I will do everything I can to justify your confidence in me," she said, a little stiffly. It was correct to address the master with formality, but the proper phrases came badly to her. "I know I am young. I know I have much to learn. My father has reminded me of this every day since I was six. He probably did so before then, but I no longer recall it. I do not need to be reminded again."

"You will also have to learn to guard your tongue. I am a liberal master, and I do not want my slaves to be silent, but there are others who are less willing to tolerate such conduct. Remember that when you are in Apollonia." He panted when he was through, as if he had been running instead of talking. "Have Minish make you some new clothes. Leather leggings and tunica if you like, but with a little more . . . dash. Have the leather dyed in bright colors, or fringed, or something so that you do not look like a stable hand. Ask Minish what she suggests. She has seen arena performers. She'll know what's best to do."

"As you wish," Tishtry said, more baffled than ever by this unexpected kindness. "Is there anything else you require of me, or am I free to finish looking after my team? They need currying."

"Take care of your team," Barantosz said with the

practicality of a man who had worked with horses for a long time. "When they are stabled and you have seen Minish, then come to my study with your father, and I will see you have a copy of the deed to your horses, as well as a proper chest to keep it in. Nothing too large, so that you may carry it with you. I'll also provide a blanket authorization that will permit you to decide how you want to perform, so that you will not find yourself having to argue at a later date." He looked at her thoughtfully. "You will have to learn more tricks, of course, but you know enough for Apollonia. If you intend to go further, you should start now to learn new tricks."

"Yes. I've been thinking about that," Tishtry said, surprised at the generosity that Barantosz was showing her. "I can jump from back to back of the team while they gallop, but I've been trying to find a way to do a somersault in the air while I leap, and then land on the next horse. I can do it coming off the back, but not going from one to another. I also want to find some way to get from the chariot onto their backs without just climbing. It seems so . . . ordinary, doing that."

"A good start," Barantosz agreed. "And you might teach the horses to do more, you know, to change paces together while you're on them, or to dance while you're in the chariot. All those things would be interesting." He tried to smile, but his face was not used to it and he ended up looking as if he had a headache or a sore tooth. "I could ask some of the other horse breeders who have charioteers, if you like, what tricks their bestiarii can do. You might learn something from—"

It was wrong for a slave to interrupt a master, but

Tishtry did. "No, not anyone here. Everyone will have seen what they can do, and will compare me to the others, and all that will happen is that I will look like a beginner, which I am. If I am to learn new tricks, I must think of them myself, or wait until I arrive in Apollonia. Nothing else will work."

"I had not considered that," Barantosz said, trying to show his approval.

"I have. It's all I've had to think about these evenings. I want to show you that I can improve."

"And show your worth so that you can earn enough to buy your family's freedom," Barantosz finished for her. "A worthy ambition for you. I have already placed the valuation with the court, and the price is fixed. I have also given my word that I will not sell any of them for a period of five years—barring bankruptcy or war, of course—so that you will have time enough to get the money needed."

Tishtry stopped walking her horses again. "Why are you being so reasonable? There are other masters who would not do this."

"There are good reasons for Armenians to cooperate with the Romans. The Romans are very strict in their slave laws, and they are not pleased when their laws are abused. I have a license to sell mules and horses to them, and the authority from our King to breed up to five hundred horses. You are a good girl, Tishtry, and your father is a good man, but none of you are worth that government license. So I will do all that I can to uphold the Roman slave laws, and be careful in my conduct. I want to have another license next year, and the year after that. It is my hope that I will have a thousand horses here in ten years, but that will not happen if the Romans do not approve of how I run my business." He nodded slowly. "So you see, girl, I have no reason to play you false. And you have every reason to do the best that you are able, so that you may free your family at last. It is in both our interests that you perform and improve." He stroked Shirdas. "Your horses are a testimony to the quality of my animals. Take good care of them."

"As you have already reminded me, it is in my best interests to do that." She lifted her chin to stare at him. "And besides, they are mine."

Barantosz made a growling sound that Tishtry knew was his way of chuckling. "You're right; they're yours."

CHAPTER

It was difficult for Tishtry to look at Soduz because she was afraid that she would cry, and that would be wrong. The four months since she had received her team had passed too quickly. She took the cup of watered wine he offered and drank the stuff down much more quickly than she usually did. "Then it is set? I leave in three days?"

"Yes. Barantosz was pleased at the report of his neighbors, and so there's no reason to keep you here. The Games at Apollonia begin in a month, and this way you will have a little time to get used to the larger arena, and the team can, too." He coughed once to clear his throat. "I said you'd be ready."

The time had gone by so fast, Tishtry thought. She had assumed it would be much longer—always in the past the months had crept by. Now she was about to leave and it seemed only a few days ago, not four months, that her master had outlined his plans for her. "I . . . I'll be ready."

"Good. There will be a group of trainers going to Apollonia for the spring bidding, and Barantosz has said that you will go with him. After you arrive in Apollonia, he will pay the fees to enter you, and from then it is up to the Master of the Bestiarii to decide where you will do the best."

"Fine." She wished that they were not alone. Her mother and her father's other wife would let her have the chance to cry.

"Macon has almost finished the saddles. She might be able to go with you." He doubted that Barantosz would be willing to stand the cost of taking another slave with him, but he could see how miserable Tishtry was, and he knew he had to make the effort, even if nothing came of it.

"I've practiced with the two she has finished," Tishtry said, hardly knowing what she meant. Being without Macon was unthinkable. She could not face losing all her family so completely.

"Good. You'll do fine in Apollonia. I have heard that the crowd there has a love of horses. Your four will please them."

"I hope so," she muttered, her mind on other things. She wanted to have a word or two with her groom, so that the horses would not be mishandled when they were got ready for the journey. "Immit is ear shy," she murmured, and let her father give her a little more wine.

"And Dozei does not like to be approached from the rear," Soduz finished for her. "I have told the grooms that. They all have heard it from you, and from me. If

28

any of them do wrong, it will not be our mistake." He put his hand on her shoulder and turned toward the orchard behind the stable. "Come, girl. Let's walk together. It's pleasant enough out."

Tishtry sighed, but allowed herself to be coaxed out into the sunlight. "I . . . I don't want to go."

"Yes, you do," Soduz said firmly. "You're afraid that you will be lonely, and I think it is likely that you will be. That's natural, my daughter, and you should not feel that you are wrong to miss us. But," he went on, not giving her any opportunity to argue this point with him, "you are going to have much to do, and there will be little time for you to feel sorry for yourself—"

"*Sorry* for myself?" she demanded.

"That is how it might appear to those who do not know you," he said in his most bracing tone. "You will have to think about your demeanor now, because you will be with many strangers, and most of them will have little reason to give you more than passing attention. It is your conduct that will make the difference, and if you drag about and look hangdog, they will ignore you, and listen to those with a more cooperative attitude. Do you understand me, girl?"

"I am supposed to put on a brave front, and—"

Her father cut her short. "No, not a brave front!" He stopped and looked down at her. "What are you? A half-grown cur prancing and fawning in the hope of finding a master? No! You are the best trick rider our family has ever had, and we have been trick riders for generations. You have only to be what you are, girl, and you will shine. I thought you'd learned the difference between courage and bravery. Any fool can show

29

bravery, but it takes courage to jump from the back of one galloping horse to the back of another, and smile while you do it. Keep *that* in mind when you meet strangers, and recall that we would not let our freedom ride on you if you were not the finest rider in this family."

To her chagrin, Tishtry began to speak, and instead burst into tears. Her face went scarlet and she tried to turn away.

"No, no, girl. There's no shame in weeping." Soduz clapped his arm around her shoulder and pulled her close to him. "You're a good girl, and a superb horse-woman, and there is no reason you cannot rise as high as anyone in the arenae of the Empire. The new Emperor likes chariot races and charioteers, and so even Roma is not beyond your grasp." He patted her in rough comfort. "You'll do us proud, I am certain of it."

She was able to make a muffled reply, but even she thought it made little sense.

Apparently this did not bother Soduz. "Come, Tishtry, let it out now, while it will trouble no one. I don't want Barantosz thinking he has made a mistake. The man is so easily flustered that we must take great care with him, so that he will not be misled." He drew her with him to a bench under the trees. "Now, girl, pay attention to me."

She wiped her eyes with the back of her hand. "Yes, Father," she sniffed.

"Barantosz will change his mind a dozen times before you reach Apollonia, and it will be up to you to remain firm in your purpose and tell him that you are eager to go on. Otherwise he will lose heart and it will be another year at least before he will be able to undertake such a venture. If he sees that you are faltering, he will abandon the whole thing, and we will be the worse for it."

"All right," she said, more confidently.

"He may be the master and we his slaves, but it will not be the first time that the slaves have made the master. Keep that thought before you and you will know how best to go on." He paused a moment, then poured her more wine from the jug he carried. "He will give many orders, of course, but you will have to keep the purpose in mind. The grooms will look to you for guidance, not Barantosz, and if you do not stay firm, there could be trouble. Remember, they are *your* horses, not Barantosz's, and you must care for them or they will suffer for it."

"I will." She felt some of the fear that had been gnawing at her leave her mind.

"And you will have to be sure that no one in Apollonia is mistaken in your purpose. You are not there to race—not that they would permit a woman to race, but still—you are there to perform, and to do tricks that none of the racing charioteers could do in a decade of practice." He stopped, and his manner softened. "I am going to miss you, girl."

This time she controlled her sobs, though she felt her eyes fill. "When you are free, Father, then perhaps we will see each other again."

"Yes," he said, and they both knew it was a lie.

"The gods will favor us," she said, aware that now he was the one who needed cheering. "It will not be long before you are free."

"I am certain of it." He stood up. "There is going to be a feast tomorrow, to honor you and to reassure our master. No sadness then, Tishtry. You must learn to smile for him."

"As I do when I jump from horse to horse?" she asked, attempting to smile for her father and failing.

"It's something like practice," he said, and Tishtry saw with amazement that Soduz, her hearty, practical father, was fighting back tears.

She set her cup aside and got to her feet. "I won't fail you, Father."

At last he had to look away. "I know."

Macon came running into the room where her family kept the tack for their horses. Her face was flushed and her eyes were bright, and when she spoke, her voice was high with excitement. "Oh, Father! Barantosz has said I'm to go with Tishtry. He didn't refuse!"

Soduz turned from his work to look at her. "You spoke to him?"

"Just now. I said that I would need time to prepare my equipment, and there is only a day to do it." She dragged one of the three-legged stools away from the wall and sat, reaching for the largest leather satchel in the room. "I'll take my gear and enough supplies to make Tishtry another saddle and bridle, so she will have a spare, in case anything happens."

"Have you told her yet?" Soduz asked. He was rubbing oil into a pair of reins, testing them for suppleness as he worked.

"Not yet. I thought I'd find her as soon as I've packed." She was gathering up supplies as she spoke, and she tried hard not to rush, knowing that she was likely to forget something if she did.

"Very good. Does your mother know?" He asked it awkwardly; it was difficult to lose two children at the same time.

"Not yet." She looked up, her expression serious. "I will *not* be sold. He gave me his word on that. I will return here." She took a half-completed wooden frame. "He knows I'm a good saddler and he doesn't want to set a value on me that will make it apparent that I have great skill. So it follows that he will keep me. That's sensible."

"He also gave his word that the family would be kept intact for five years, so that Tishtry might have the chance to earn enough to free us." He said it slowly, wondering if it would be possible. Tishtry had done her best to appear confident, but in the last day, Soduz was beginning to doubt their chances.

"Then I will be returning," Macon said calmly. "And there is no reason to fear." She picked up two scrapers. "Which one shall I leave for you?"

"The bone-handled one," Soduz answered.

Macon went on with her packing, then said, "I wish now that one of us could read and write. That way, we could send word to you that all is well, and inform everyone of how Tishtry is doing."

"I couldn't read the message in any case," Soduz told her.

"Yes, but there are those here who could, and that way . . . well, it doesn't matter. Whoever learned to read in less than a day?" Macon sighed as she looked around the room. "I need thongs and twine. Where are they?"

"Second shelf under the window. Leave some for me," Soduz said, then gave her a long, steady look. "Guard yourself, child, and your sister. Slaves are vulnerable, and you are woman enough for men to want you."

"That's for Barantosz to say," Macon reminded her father.

"Still, you should take care. Barantosz isn't one to protest too much for his slaves." He shook his head. "When the time comes, I hope he'll choose well for you, Macon."

"So do I," Macon answered wistfully. "Tishtry's safe enough—no woman rides well carrying a child, let alone does tricks, and that's her value to our master. He won't let Tishtry be any man's woman as long as she can win for him in the arena. If she ever wants a man for herself, she'll have a hard time convincing Barantosz to allow it." She gave a short, wise laugh. "As long as I'm with her, he'll make sure I'm safe enough. He's too nervous to risk letting either one of us find a man for a while."

"Perhaps," her father said. "But have a care in any case."

"Do you think any man we're likely to meet will be foolish enough to hazard the penalties for abusing a slave? Barantosz will take care to see we're guarded."

"I think that many men are foolish where women are concerned, and women where men are," Soduz said. "And the penalties for slave abuse won't stop a fool." He nodded to himself. "You're a clever girl, like your sister, but you've got sense enough to be cautious. That benefits you, but it hinders you as well. If only Tishtry weren't quite as impetuous as she is." He fell silent. "Macon, if we were free, it wouldn't matter. But until we are, we must be practical and sensible at all times. You know that, even if Tishtry doesn't."

Macon came to his side. "You're saying that you'll worry about us," she corrected him. "Father, at least we're not being sold."

Soduz chuckled ruefully. "You're right. I am worried."

"I will thank the gods for your care," Macon promised him, then lifted her satchel with difficulty.

"You're carrying a lot," Soduz remarked, trying to make light of their parting.

"You taught me that I should always have what I need on hand," Macon said, then kissed his cheek. "I'll come back, Father. I will."

Soduz patted her hand, but said nothing.

It was a blustery morning when Barantosz gathered his little cavalcade together and started out for Apollonia. Most of the household came out to bid them a safe journey and to wish them well in the venture.

"I will send word back, my word on it," Tishtry called out to her mother, waving for the entire gathering to see. She knew that her father was depending on her to show enthusiasm and eagerness, so she resolutely kept the tears from her eyes and determinedly smiled and called out encouragement to those around her. Mounted on Shirdas, she let the chestnut curvet and sidle, showing his mettle; she felt his tension through the reins, and kept her hands light. "Have a care!"

"The gods favor you!" Soduz shouted, gesturing to the rest of his family to wave heartily. "Do us honor!"

Tishtry held up her hand to them, accepting this charge with purpose. "I will!"

Barantosz, riding in a biga pulled by matched blacks, came abreast of her and scowled. "I want you to take the second place in line, behind me."

He was showing her unusual courtesy, and Tishtry was confused at his order. "The second place?"

"You're the main reason we're going. You should be in the second place." He turned to glower at his charioteer. "And don't go too fast. You know that the roads are not all good. I don't want a broken wheel or axle for our efforts."

The charioteer, a whip-slender Greek, just shrugged. He looked across at Tishtry. "They're bringing your quadriga and the rest of your team up behind you. I'll hold to a trot most of the way."

"All right," Tishtry responded, feeling the first welling of pride. It was not as painful to leave her family if it was done with distinction like this. "I will keep to a trot."

"Your team is five-paced?" the Greek asked.

"Of course," Tishtry answered haughtily. "You've seen them work."

"Then we will expect them to do the uphill gait when we enter Apollonia." He nodded with Barantosz as he said it. "They should attract some attention that way."

"We won't be at Apollonia until tomorrow afternoon," Tishtry reminded the two men. "We can work out our plans when we stop for the night." She realized she was being high-handed in her conduct, but her father had told her several times that she must take a positive stance with Barantosz. "I don't know what the

36

road is like there, and if there is a crowd, it might be better just to get through the gates as best we can."

"A good thought," Barantosz said, and began to toy with the ends of his belt. "We would not want to cause any difficulties, since the Guard might not permit us to bring the horses inside the walls if—"

The Greek whipped up the blacks, and the last of Barantosz's dithering was lost in the rumble of wheels and the clapping of hooves.

Four wagons back, Macon sat with three other women behind the driver. The vehicle was uncomfortable and the big mules that pulled it were bad tempered, but Macon bore it all with calm good humor. She watched her younger sister riding ahead, and felt gratitude to Tishtry for making the journey possible for her. She had never complained to her family, but for three years she had longed to get away from the limited world of Barantosz's land. For a slave there was little choice, and often the alternatives were unpleasant. But now Macon was getting her wish, and without the distress of being sold.

Tishtry grinned, thinking of all the wonderful stories she could tell when she returned. She wanted to convince herself that she would return, no matter how remote the chance, since it made leaving bearable. It was hard enough to go when she wanted to think of her return, but if she did not come back, it would be agony to leave. She shook herself inwardly, telling herself that it was foolish to be troubled. Before she let herself be distressed by such questions, she would have to succeed in the arena. If she won, there would be sweetenings given to her by those who made money from her performances, and there would be time then to think about when she could return.

Tishtry took her place behind Barantosz's biga and reluctantly pulled Shirdas to a trot. The chestnut tossed his head in protest, then steadied into the pace as Tishtry's quadriga was brought up behind her, driven by one of the older grooms. Dust blew around them, swirling and stinging. Tishtry ignored it, keeping her mind instead on her master's chariot, ahead of her on the road to Apollonia.

CHAPTER

IV

For the first ten rows, the seats of the amphitheater at Apollonia were made of marble, but beyond that there were wooden benches on bricks. The oblong structure could accommodate more than five thousand spectators and was by far the largest arena Tishtry had ever seen. She stood by the Gates of Life and stared at the enormous place.

On the sands there were three charioteers taking their teams on practice runs around the course, each of them maneuvering close to the long partition down the middle of the arena, a low brick wall called the spina. There were wooden fenders at either end of the spina, all showing countless impact scars. These were the metae, and as Tishtry watched, one of the charioteers cut in too close and his quadriga grazed the nearest meta, leaving yet another mark on the wood.

Chimbue Barantosz had the fidgets, which surprised no one but himself. He paced along the wall of the amphitheater, paying little attention to the charioteers, his Greek driver walking beside him. "I was told that the Master of the Bestiarii would meet me an hour ago. Where is the man? Where *is* he?"

Tishtry, enjoying the view from her vantage point, did not listen to her master's protests. She was too caught up in the excitement of the arena to be worried by his constant fussing.

"He was *supposed* to be here," Barantosz insisted, raising his voice.

"You are Chimbue Barantosz?" someone spoke up from behind him.

The three turned toward the questioner. "Who are you?" Barantosz demanded of the lean and angular young man who regarded them so confidently.

"Master of the Bestiarii" was the answer. "You were supposed to meet me in the training arena, weren't you?"

"You sent word that you would meet me at the arena; we came here." Barantosz was feeling abused, and he could not resist the impulse to pout. "You kept us waiting."

"I would not have if you had come to the training arena," the man said. "I am called Atadillius, Barantosz."

"Atadillius," Barantosz repeated as if the name tasted bad. "Very well. I am here with my slave." He nodded toward Tishtry. "You were sent word about her."

Atadillius regarded Tishtry with some surprise. "You're

very young," he said at last, as if he had to say something.

"That doesn't matter," Tishtry responded, though Atadillius' confidence was a little daunting to her.

"Perhaps not. Are you reckless?"

There was no way to tell what sort of answer he wanted from that unexpected question, so Tishtry glanced at her master and then said, "I'm careful of my horses, and I don't plan to let myself get hurt."

Atadillius gave a brief, fierce smile. "I see." He turned his attention to Barantosz. "When can I see what she does?"

Barantosz scowled. "There are the horses to see to, and if they are recovered from the journey, it might be possible . . . before sunset, if it is urgent." The last came out in a rush and he looked uneasily toward Tishtry. "If you think you can do it?"

"There should be no problem," she said, secretly amazed that she should sound so sure of herself.

"At the training arena then, an hour before sunset." He looked down into the arena, his expression critical. "Paiden is getting sloppy. It happens when you get too old."

Tishtry, who had been watching the charioteers closely, asked, "Is he the one with the grays?"

There was a hint of respect in Atadillius' manner now. "What makes you think so?"

"Well, he's feathered the metae three times in the last five circuits, and the other two haven't." She pointed to the chariot. "You see? He's going to do it again."

The impact of wheel on meta was a loud crack and

41

the chariot teetered around the end of the spina, visibly wobbling.

"He'll lose the wheel on the next turn," Tishtry predicted.

"The shock wasn't *that* bad," Atadillius protested.

"Yes it was," Tishtry declared. "It will collapse when he tries to lean into the turn." She was certain of what she said, and found his doubt irritating. "If he leans with the chariot, he'll go over."

Atadillius folded his arms and sighed. "All right. Let's watch."

Barantosz could sense the challenge between the Master of the Bestiarii and his slave. He pulled unhappily at the ends of his belt and tried to think of a comment that would calm the two. "You don't know what chariots will do" was the best he could come up with.

Below them, Paiden leaned in his chariot as it approached the end of the spina. Slowly the wheel slipped on its axle, folding farther under the vehicle with each rotation. Realizing too late that he was in danger, Paiden tried to shift his weight, but his last-second efforts were useless; the wheel broke free and the quadriga lurched onto its side, spilling Paiden onto the sands. The three yoked horses were able to drag the chariot a little way, but the free-running inside horse took the bit in his teeth and in a sudden burst of speed snapped his traces.

"Well?" Tishtry said, looking toward Atadillius.

"He lost the wheel," the Master of the Bestiarii acknowledged. "You must have been watching closely."

"*Anyone* could have seen that was going to happen," Tishtry scoffed, enjoying her little victory.

"Just see that you do as well in the practice arena," Atadillius said coldly.

As Atadillius stalked off, Barantosz looked after him, misery in his eyes. "I hope he'll still let you perform here, that's all I can say."

Tishtry grinned.

It was the third time that Tishtry had been asked to go through her routine in the practice arena, and by now she was beginning to feel comfortable in the larger space. In the four days since she had arrived, she had become an object of curiosity, which pleased her. She noticed that there were more than a dozen people sitting on the fence around the practice arena, and she smiled as she led her horses onto the sands. She saluted her audience, then climbed into her quadriga, flipping the reins to put her team in motion. She felt the familiar strength of the horses in the pull on her arms as the team went from walk to trot to canter.

On the fence, Atadillius nodded to himself as Tishtry made her first circuit of the arena. He admired the way she handled her horses and he liked her style, no matter how clumsy and undeveloped it was.

"What are you thinking?" Macon asked from her place beside him.

"With a little development, she might be worth sending to a bigger arena," Atadillius answered as he turned to smile at Tishtry's sister.

Macon was not able to smile in return. "There are more risks in bigger arenae, aren't there." She hesitated. "Our brother was killed doing tricks in his quadriga, and I am afraid it will happen to her, as well."

"Not a chance," Atadillius assured her. "I've been watching her, and no matter what it might look like, she takes no chances at all."

Now that the team had settled into their steady, smooth gallop, Tishtry climbed out of the chariot, springing onto Dozei's back and crouching there until the horses thundered out of the tight turn at the end of the circuit and had a long, straight stretch ahead of them. This was the part she liked best, the exhilaration of that first stand. When she was younger it had frightened her, but now she was so used to the trick and to her team that the fear had almost left her. She rose up and raised her arms over her head, fists clenched, as her father had taught her.

"It's a good beginning," Atadillius said, "but there's nothing special about it. She should find a way to make more of it."

"Isn't standing on the back of a running horse enough?" Macon asked, a bit shocked to hear Tishtry criticized.

"Not for Romans, no," Atadillius answered. "She should have a little more to make it really special, bring it to the attention of the crowd. The way she does that, you'd think anyone could do it. The thing is for her to do something that makes it clear that although it is easy enough for her, no one else could manage it." He pointed to the quadriga. "She needs a better chariot as well, one that lets her do more with it."

"Our master isn't likely to buy her one, and she has yet to make any more money from her performances to purchase one herself," Macon pointed out.

"We'll see." Atadillius braced his elbows on his knees

and leaned forward on the fence, watching closely as Tishtry began to jump lightly from the back of one horse to another. "I wish she'd skip."

"*Skip?*" Macon repeated in astonishment.

"Well, that or something more unusual." He rested his chin on his laced fingers. "Pity the team isn't a matched one."

"It *is*," Macon insisted.

"I meant for color. Still, better that they are the same size and have the same stride, I suppose, given what she does." He pointed to the little saddle on Amath, the dark bay. "Did you make that?"

"Of course. And the bridles," Macon said, with a touch of pride. "I make all the saddles and bridles for the family."

As if to thank her older sister for the saddle, Tishtry bent down, grasped the special handholds on the fenders of the saddle, then extended herself in a handstand as the horses continued to race around the practice arena.

Several of those on the fence who had been watching her silently now applauded and hooted their approval.

"That's one of her best tricks," Atadillius conceded. "I've never seen anyone do that before. Still, if she could find another trick, even more spectacular, then it would be wonderful."

Tishtry braced herself as she came out of the handstand. Then she sprang into the air, somersaulting backward to land on her feet in the quadriga, where she once again took the reins and guided her team on a last sweep around the arena. That was the only part of the routine that worried her. Her quadriga, being a standard racing chariot, was badly balanced for the trick, and once she had twisted her ankle on landing. She had a few ideas about how her vehicle could be made better.

The gates at the end of the practice arena opened and she shot through them, noting with satisfaction that several of the grooms had stopped their work to take a peek at her performance.

"You did quite well," Atadillius said as he came up to her when she had got out of the chariot and was helping to unhitch her team.

"I know," she answered. "And I will do better. I want to make the routine longer, but the horses aren't ready for that yet. I don't know what they'll be like when the amphitheater is full. All the people and noise may make them nervous."

"It could," Atadillius agreed. "We'll find out next week."

"So soon?" Macon wanted to know. Her face, usually thoughtful and calm, was now creased with worry. "Shouldn't she have more time?"

"So that other charioteers may come and watch her and try to get the advantage of her by doing her tricks before she does them?" Atadillius asked. "I'm going to talk to Barantosz tonight. We'll arrange it."

"Good," Tishtry said, then added, "They may try to do my tricks if they like. It took most of my life for me to learn them, and if they think they can master them overnight, let them do their best."

Atadillius shook his head. "No doubt what you say is true, but don't repeat it; others may hear you and take it for a challenge. Time enough for that when you

46

are well established and there are editoris trying to place you in their Games.''

''All right.'' Tishtry finished the unhitching and called to one of the grooms, ''I'm going to walk them.''

''Your master would do well to purchase an aurigatore for you, to help you with the care of your animals and your equipment. Rivals have been known to sabotage one another through the use of stable hands.'' Atadillius rubbed his chin. ''Would you look after her tack, Macon, until we find someone right? It's not what you are trained for, and it might be that your master will not like it, but it would be wiser.''

Macon nodded. ''I don't want to see anything happen to Tishtry. I'll be pleased to look after her tack.''

''I think you're both being worse than nursemaids, but if you want to go to all this trouble, who am I to stop you?'' Tishtry said, and led her horses away toward the open area where she could walk her team.

Chimbue Barantosz took a hasty gulp of wine. ''How do you mean, it would be possible for Tishtry to go further?''

Atadillius favored him with a superior smile. ''You have a remarkable young slave there, Barantosz, and it is a shame you have been so shortsighted about what she might accomplish, given the chance.'' He dropped onto one of the dining couches and helped himself to the spiced pork set out on the table between them. ''I'm surprised you haven't thought of it yourself.'' This last was a lie, but Atadillius was sure it would serve his purpose.

''I never thought that . . . well, she's quite good, I

suppose, but . . . she's very young, after all." He had some more wine. "Her family are quite hopeful for her, but . . ."

Atadillius did not let Barantosz dither any longer. "Small wonder. I have been Master of the Bestiarii since I bought my freedom six years ago, and I tell you that never have I seen a girl work horses the way Tishtry does. She lacks polish and she needs instruction in performing, but knowing what she can do, I am convinced that she might eventually make it as far as Roma, and the Circus Maximus."

"Gods of the fishes!" Barantosz burst out, his soft, babyish features turning rosy and his mouth opening in astonishment. "Tishtry? In Roma?"

"It's possible. With care and good sense." He paused, then went on even more smoothly as he reached for more pork, "It will take time, and I would want your assurance that I have the right to work with her, coach her and all."

"It will cost me money, won't it?" Barantosz cut in.

"Naturally. But once the winter storms come, there will be plenty of time to practice and perfect her tricks. There are no Games here in the winter, and that means a good three months to devote to making her performance better."

"But the cost . . ." Barantosz persisted.

"If she improves—and I believe she will—you could sell her for a great deal of money. You wouldn't have to risk more than you'd have to invest in my time and abilities. That wouldn't put you at a disadvantage for long." He assumed a more casual manner as he grew confident of his success. Barantosz, he knew, was as

48

greedy as he was timid, so he added, "I'd be willing to take part of my pay in commission from her sale."

At that, Barantosz looked up, a flicker of interest in his hooded eyes. "How great a part?"

"Thirty percent," Atadillius said.

"Fifty percent," Barantosz countered at once. "If you will defer half of your payment contingent on her sale, well, then it might be arranged." He plucked at the knots of his belt. "I want you to explain this to her. Let her see that it will be to her advantage in the long run."

Atadillius had heard Macon speak of the various assurances Barantosz had given Tishtry and her family. "If you wish."

"She's . . . difficult. It would be better coming from you. She'd listen to you." He took his cup and gulped some wine. "You're a practical man, Atadillius. You can make her understand."

"But why should I?" he asked innocently. "Perhaps, if you were to compromise at forty percent, I'd find myself more eloquent."

"All right." Barantosz squirmed. "Forty percent. But I don't want to have anything to do with what you say to her. Is that acceptable?"

Atadillius took the last of the pork. "Done," he said with his mouth full.

Tishtry thought she had never heard so much noise before in her life. It was worse than the howling of wind in a winter storm, and all it was was the voices of people gathered in the amphitheater to watch the Games. She had tried to pretend that she was used to it when it had first begun, but now she let herself be amazed. She was troubled that her team would bolt at the sound, for they might be frightened by it. It was not easy for her to admit to herself that it frightened her.

"Don't worry," a rangy Persian secutor said to her as he strolled by, swinging his weapons. "This is a small place. Nothing like the big arenae where there are ten times this number of people in the stands, and the sound makes you deaf after a while."

"There can't be ten times this number of people in the whole world," Tishtry protested.

The secutor laughed. "This is a small place. It might

be bigger than anything you've got back home in Cappadocia or Armenia or wherever it is you come from, but don't doubt it—this is nothing."

"But it's . . . so much." She thought of her tricks, hoping she would be able to do them for the gigantic crowd. With so many people, would any of them actually see what it was she was doing? She fingered the small brass studs that had been added to her leather costume, and she was glad now she had chosen them instead of colors, because the sunlight would make them shine, and more of the crowd would see her. She swallowed hard and tried to forget how nervous she was.

"Just do your tricks. Don't think about the people. They'll want to see what you can do. Think of this as practice, for when you get into a proper arena with twenty thousand in the stands." The secutor cuffed her shoulder in encouragement.

"Twenty thousand!" she scoffed, determined not to let the secutor get the better of her. She had learned that the veteran arena performers enjoyed gulling the newcomers with ridiculous tall stories. "You're outrageous."

"A lot you know of it, girl," the secutor chuckled. "Wait until you get to Roma."

"I will," Tishtry promised him, wondering if she would ever get to Roma to perform in the Circus Maximus, where the greatest Games in the Empire were held for more than a hundred days out of every year. She went about her tasks with her team, cleaning their hooves and inspecting them for any signs of damage, then stretching out each horse's legs, pulling them slowly, extending them to help the animals limber up. When she was satisfied, she signaled for a groom to help her yoke them up. "Be careful of Immit. She's a little head shy."

The groom stared at the silver-dun mare as if daring her to misbehave. "I've yoked up lions, girl. There aren't many horses that are too much for me."

"That may be," Tishtry said sharply, "but you may be too much for her. She has to be on the sands shortly and that crowd is bad enough. If you vex her now, then we may do badly." She took the bridle out of the groom's hands. "I had better do it myself."

Atadillius, who had been watching this exchange, took a moment to stroll over to the young Armenian. "Very wise, Tishtry."

"Don't you start on me," Tishtry countered as she fixed the bit in Shirdas' mouth.

"I'm not starting on you," Atadillius protested with what appeared to be genuine concern. "There are those who would prefer you fail today, and there are many ways to accomplish that. Take care, girl. You are not amusing your master's friends at home anymore, you are a bestiarii in the amphitheater at Apollonia. Remember that. Fortunes are made and lost on these Games."

Tishtry shrugged. "That is the worry of the gamblers," she said, dismissing the matter.

"And suppose that gambler has put money on you, to win or to lose. Do you think that they would stop at hurting a few horses or an unknown slave? At the moment, it would cost little to compensate your master for your market value, and there are some who would find that an excellent investment."

52

"They're fools," Tishtry said as she tightened the last of the buckles.

"Possibly. But just the same, stay near the spina, so that they cannot throw things at you." Atadillius hesitated, puzzled by Tishtry's attitude. "Word has spread about you, girl. There are men in the stands who have been speculating about you, with denarii."

At this mention of money, Tishtry looked up at him, curious for the first time. She wished she could still the sudden rush of stage fright that had taken hold of her. "They're betting on *me*? But why? I don't race, I just drive and ride."

"And perhaps you might fall, or you might do a trick they haven't seen before," Atadillius suggested. "Have a care, girl. Your sister would never pardon me if I let you be hurt here."

Tishtry tossed her head, more nervous than ever. "What has my sister to do with this?" Her interest was piqued by this turn of their conversation, but her apprehension kept her from asking anything more.

"Go ride. Then have her explain it to you." With that, Atadillius strode abruptly away.

Just before the Gates of Life were opened, Tishtry got into her chariot and tried to whisper a few reassurances to her team, but gave up when she found herself almost shouting to be heard. She tried to calm herself, afraid that her nervousness would communicate itself to her horses, and they would be more keyed up than they were already. She forced herself to take a few deep breaths and be calm. "It's just like home," she said to herself. "This crowd is no different from the horse breeders and wine makers. There's just more of them." She cleared her throat, surprised at how tight it had become.

The brazen hoots of the hydraulic organ ended and the aurigatore standing at the heads of her team signaled her as the Gates of Life swung open.

Tishtry gathered up the traces and stretched her mouth into a smile as she sent her horses hurtling out onto the sands.

A sound between a buzz and a roar greeted her appearance, and Tishtry watched her teams' ears turn back. She felt her hands shaking and she forced them to be still. It was bad enough to have her team so upset, but for her to be as distressed as they went beyond anything she could accept. She set her jaw and put her mind on her tricks.

Her first vault onto Dozei's back brought applause, and this startled her so much she almost lost her footing. She did her best to turn her near-stumble into a kind of jig, and kept up this impromptu little dance for one whole circuit of the arena. She discovered that this was soothing to her, making her less distracted by the noise around her. She nodded once to herself and put her mind on her next trick. The noise around her became less demanding, and she decided that she could continue her ride without too much difficulty. She started her bounce from horse to horse and felt a certain satisfaction that this time the enthusiasm of the crowd did not shatter her concentration.

On Atadillius' suggestion, Tishtry kept her first appearance brief, doing only those tricks she had the greatest experience performing. Her confidence improved, and the crowd loved it.

In less than a week, she and her team were back on the sands once more. This time she did a few more of her tricks, but not her handstand. She argued with Atadillius about it, but he remained firm.

"Your horses are still skittish from the noise, you can't deny that," he reminded her. "And that would mean you might do badly. Not doing a trick at all is better than doing it badly. You have all summer to get ready for it. By fall, you will have a routine twice as long as the one you do now, and the sweetenings the editor pays you will more than double. Everyone will think that you are improving before their eyes—which you are, but not the way they will assume—and that will increase the fee paid for your performances."

That last was powerfully persuasive, since the sweetenings and the small portion that was her share of the performance fees would go toward buying her family's freedom. Tishtry was quite pleased to have amassed a pouchful of silver denarii and an assortment of copper coins, some Roman, some Greek. "How much more?"

"Double," he said confidently. "If your reputation spreads, possibly more."

Tishtry laughed. "My reputation?"

"You're getting one. Now is the time you must have a care. I'll tell Barantosz, so he'll take extra care of you."

"Very well." Tishtry chuckled, convinced that Atadillius was being absurdly cautious.

Yet by midsummer she had had one trace snap on her while she was working with Shirdas, and had discovered that the leather had been deeply cut with a knife. And not long after, she had noticed that the spokes of her quadriga had been tampered with. She became more cautious.

August was difficult, for the engulfing heat was worsened by hot, dry winds blowing in from Asia. Everyone in the arena turned surly, even her horses, and Tishtry, for the first time in her life, wanted to avoid performing with her team.

"Tell Barantosz that you are ill," Macon suggested as they sat in the cabin, both of them half dressed and sweating.

"But I am not ill, and he has already been paid for my appearance. He hates to give back money. Atadillius . . . he thinks that it might be better if I perform because there are others who are going to refuse. That Boeotian bestiarii with the tigers has already said he cannot trust his cats in this heat." She looked directly at Macon. "I could earn a lot, working these Games."

"And you could lose a lot too," her older sister reminded her. "You are not so favored by the gods that you may fly in the face of fate."

"I will not do that," Tishtry said with a weary smile. "I will do a shorter version of my tricks and it will be enough."

"If you're sure," Macon said doubtfully.

"Well, I think I am," she responded. "But there must be enough water for the horses when I am through, and I will need a long time to walk them cool, otherwise they could be harmed, and I draw the line at that."

Three other bestiarii withdrew from the Games during the hot winds, and as a result, Tishtry was one of the specialty entertainments. She created more excitement with her performance because there were few bestiarii, and she decided to take full advantage of this, introducing a new trick to her routine: she somersaulted across the backs of all four horses as they galloped, and having reached Shirdas' back this way, she did a back-flip that landed her on Dozei once again. The crowd went wild for it, and the editor of the Games awarded her a sweetening of fifty silver denarii.

"You see," she boasted to Macon that evening while they ate figs and chopped mutton, "I said it would be all right, and here we are, richer than ever before."

"The money is not the most important thing," Macon warned her.

"It might not be, but there is no other way to gain your freedom and the freedom of our family. Barantosz might be a fool, but he's not so much of a fool that he'll grant his slaves their freedom on a whim. He expects money for his writ of manumission."

"The family wouldn't mind if you didn't succeed," Macon pointed out.

"*I* would mind," Tishtry said stubbornly, and despite her youth, there was no doubting her determination.

"Then be wise, so that you can achieve your goal," Macon said, then changed the subject. "Your tunica is getting worn. Would you like me to repair it?"

"Can you do that?" Tishtry asked, genuinely surprised.

"Well, leather is leather, and whether I'm making a saddle or repairing a tunica, there shouldn't be much difference, should there? I could put a few more studs on the tunica while I'm at it."

"All right. I think I'd like a sunburst design. Could you do that?" She grinned at her older sister. "Something that catches the light."

"If that's what you want," Macon said, trying not to giggle. "A sunburst it will be."

"There are two more Games scheduled between now and the end of October," Atadillius told Tishtry when she came in from her morning practice. "You've been asked for both of them. One of those asking to be editor is a Roman. His name is Marius Balbo, and he will pay very well for your performance, so save your best tricks for him. Barantosz has said that you must do something very unusual."

"What about the handstand? I've only done it once, and you know how the crowd roared for it." She grinned eagerly. "That would be sure to please Balbo, and it will please Barantosz."

Atadillius winked. "Your master has good reason to flatter the Romans; they buy most of his horses and mules."

"Fine. Then I will do what I can." She was brushing down her team's coats, going over the hair until it was free of dust. "They like this best, I think. They're as bad as cats."

"They're much bigger than cats," Atadillius observed. "Don't be too obvious with Balbo. He has that Roman tendency to like flattery unless he knows that's what it is, and then he hates it." He folded his arms. "Barantosz has given me permission to work with you in the winter, strengthening your routine."

"So I can keep the crowds coming next year?" Tishtry asked with a sigh. "If you think it's wise, I suppose I ought to do it."

Finally Atadillius could keep the idea to himself no longer. "No, not so you can keep the crowd here happy next year. Next year, if you work well, we will take you to another amphitheater. How would you like to perform in the arena at Troas?"

"Troas?" Tishtry stopped brushing. "Do you mean that?"

"Naturally. I know better than to offer you base coin, Tishtry. I think that if you take a little more time and work very hard, you will be appreciated in Troas even more than you have been here."

Tishtry frowned. "I will have to convince Barantosz that it would be worth his while to do it." The prospect of trying to persuade her master to spend more money was not pleasant, and she shook her head. "I don't know if I can."

"I'll take care of that part," Atadillius assured her. "He will listen to me because he knows that I know the Games."

"I hope so. He's been getting more nervous of late. He told one of the other charioteers that he wants to see a better return on me." She cocked her head to the side. "You're not trying to trick him, are you? He's a strange little man, but he has an ugly temper when tried, and he's been vindictive."

It was obvious that Atadillius doubted this. "I won't give him cause."

"See that you don't. You're a freedman, but I'm still a slave, and if he decides to send me home, there's nothing I can do about it. If he sends me home, that's the end of it—I don't have enough money to buy my freedom, let alone the freedom of my family. As long as I wear a collar, I can't choose for myself."

"True, but as long as you wear a collar, you can perform in the arena. Once you're free, those days are over," Atadillius reminded her. "Slaves and convicts only are permitted to appear in the arena."

Tishtry nodded. "I don't mind that part. When I have done all that I can, I will buy my freedom and . . . oh, I don't know. If I've done well enough, I suppose I could hire out as a trainer, or set myself up as a trick riding teacher. But I'd have to do more than perform here for that to work, wouldn't I?"

"Probably," Atadillius said carefully, giving Tishtry a measuring look. "You're ambitious, are you?"

She did not answer at once; she had not considered the question before. "I suppose I am. At first it was enough to earn the money to free my family, and myself, later on, but not so much anymore. When I think of my performing days ending here, I get angry, and not just because it would mean I'd be a slave all my life."

"Those can be dangerous thoughts, girl," Atadillius warned her. "They can get you into trouble."

"Yes"—she put her hands on her hips—"I *know* that, Atadillius. That's why I warned you about Barantosz. If he guessed that I want more than he wants to give me, I'd be back in Cappadocia before the moon was full again."

Atadillius sighed. "I'll be cautious. I've said that I would be." He paused a moment, then said, "What if he were to sell you, what then?"

"It would depend on who bought me," Tishtry answered. "It's his right to sell me, after all, no matter what he said before."

"Suppose you had a master who wanted to take you to the larger arenae, would you object?" His dark eyes fixed on one of her horses, as if he were afraid to look at her.

"It wouldn't be my place to object," Tishtry answered, hardly thinking about the question.

"But is that what you want?" Atadillius persisted.

"Of course. Who would not? But it's for Barantosz to send me." She looked at Atadillius with new curiosity. "Why do you ask? Is he thinking of selling me?"

"I don't know. I don't have a reason," he answered vaguely, directing his attention to the nearest railing. "When winter's over, we'll speak of this again." He started to walk away, then saw Macon approaching, and turned toward her. "I've been speaking with your little sister; she's a very canny girl."

"A family trait," Macon remarked, dimples appearing in her cheeks. "She's more outspoken than the rest of us, that's all."

Atadillius smiled, and this time his smile changed his face, made it more pleasant, almost boyish. "You're not going to claim that you're as bad as she is, surely."

"The way she talks," Macon said affectionately, "you'd think she'd been born free."

"I'm not that bad," Tishtry said, and did not linger to hear the banter. She led her horses off to the stable, where she could take time to go over their bodies, searching for any sign of welt or swelling that might mean hurt to the horses and the possibility of harm to

61

her. She thought of the winter ahead, and could not bring herself to stop worrying about what her master might do at the end of it. She knew that Atadillius was up to something, and for that reason, in spite of his assurances, Tishtry knew it would take very little to convince Barantosz that he had made a mistake in bringing her to Apollonia; and should that happen, she would doubtless be sent back to her father and the life she had led there. No matter how she tried, she could not resign herself to that idea; she was determined to go on as a performer.

CHAPTER

VI

All during the winter months, Tishtry drilled with her team, going over her routines, perfecting the tricks she knew and developing new ones. Atadillius watched her and was stern in his instructions, making her strive for a more theatrical style and a better sequence of presentation. On her own, Tishtry worked with each of her horses on a lunge, drilling the four animals as rigorously as she was being drilled herself. Although she rarely admitted it, she was enjoying herself tremendously.

Not long after the Saturnalia and the start of the New Year, Atadillius sent for Tishtry, offering her a cup of hot spiced wine. "Sit down. We have to talk."

Tishtry dropped into the nearest chair and leaned back, crossing her legs at the ankle. "What do we have to talk about?"

"Barantosz is planning to return home at the beginning of next week. We must convince him before he leaves that you are ready to go on to Troas." He held out a dish of walnuts and raisins. "Have some."

"All right," Tishtry said, taking a handful. "How do you know he's planning to leave? Has he said so?"

"He's told his grooms to prepare for travel. And Macon was told that she must have new reins and traces ready by the end of the week. Therefore our time is short. How are your new routines coming along? Have you mastered that spin on Shirdas' rump yet? The one with the flag you were working on?"

"Well," she hedged, "it's coming along, but it isn't perfect. I think that the soles of my boots irritate his coat when I do it. I've asked Macon to try to make me another pair with softer soles, more flexible. They won't last as long, but if they're more pliant, it'll be worth it for many reasons." She popped a few of the raisins and nuts into her mouth. "Do you know what made my master want to leave? Has he said anything about it to you?"

Atadillius shrugged. "I think it was that Roman, Balbo, who was talking about a new horse breeder he's found. Barantosz's afraid that it might mean a loss of business for him—that's absurd, of course—and he's got himself convinced that he must take action at once or be without buyers for his stock."

"I see." There was no way she could admit to Atadillius how great a blow this was for her. She felt a dull pain behind her eyes, as if she had been in the sun too long; her throat was oddly stiff, so that when she talked, she sounded like an old woman. "He would be troubled if he thought he'd been deprived of a market."

"Don't be worried, Tishtry," Atadillius said, seeing how distressed she was. "I'm sure I can convince him of the need for you to go on. Or perhaps I can find a new master for you. That would be one solution, wouldn't it?"

"But who'd take the chance?" Tishtry said miserably.

"There might be someone," Atadillius said with a smooth smile. "It could be worked out, with a little luck. Burn a pinch of incense to Tyche and see if she doesn't show you favor. I'll start making inquiries for you, all right?" He poured them both a little more wine. "Your sister will help you, that's certain."

"What can she do?" Tishtry asked, feeling the icy touch of hopelessness. "Barantosz can be a very determined man. If he's decided we're going home, then there's nothing I can do to change that."

"And you're not a very determined girl?" Atadillius asked with such an air of complete innocence that Tishtry laughed in spite of her falling spirits.

"Oh, I know what I want, but I'm a slave, and that takes my life out of my hands. You remember what it's like, don't you? I know Barantosz said I'd have five years, but it's not binding, since there's no formal contract." This gloomy thought took hold of her, and she stared into the middle distance as if the answer might lie just out of sight.

"You let me talk to him, and you can be certain that we'll have you on your way to Troas. My word on it. And since I'm a freedman, my word has some worth." He got up. "I'll need a few days, and if you can avoid talking with your master until after I've had a chance to reason with him, we might carry it off."

"All right. I'll keep silent if I can. But if he sends for me, you know I must come," she said, sighing. "I was hoping there would be more time."

"There will be," Atadillius said.

"I could learn so much more, and I'm just starting to know how to perform for a large crowd. It's hard to give it up."

Atadillius shook his head in exasperation. "Will you *listen* to me? I think he can be persuaded. Do you understand that? Do you?"

"Yes," she said softly. "But I dare not get my hopes up."

This somber realization took some of the confidence out of Atadillius, who reached over and tousled Tishtry's short-cropped hair. "I know; I know."

Barantosz came puffing through the stable yard, his dumpy body swathed in three woolen dalmaticae to keep out the winter chill. "You! Tishtry! Come here!" He toddled quickly toward her when he caught sight of her team.

"Master?" Tishtry said, trying to appear casual while her courage sank down to her knees. "What is it?"

"I've been speaking to that Atadillius fellow. The—"

"Master of the Bestiarii," Tishtry finished for him. "What about?"

"You *know* what about, girl. I'll have none of that pretense from you!" His face darkened and his fat little hands were bunched into fists. "You've been talking with him, I know you have."

"Naturally. He has been coaching me," Tishtry admitted, trying not to hold the reins too tight, for that would frighten her horses more than the tone of her voice was already disturbing them.

"And he's been saying things about Troas and other arenae, hasn't he? That's what he wanted to talk to me about, Troas!" He looked around to see if they were being watched, and noticing that several of the grooms had stopped, he lowered his voice. "I hear you're ambitious. I hear you want to go to the Circus Maximus in Roma. What is the matter with you?"

"Nothing," Tishtry answered, not caring if she angered Barantosz with her candor. "Atadillius has encouraged me, and I know that I am improving. Why should I not go to Troas and Roma?" She reached up to pat Immit's neck in reassurance.

"By all the gods of thunder and horses, what possessed you?" He glowered at her. "You're being disobedient, and you've spoken against me. You know I could have you flogged for that." He paced, waiting for an explanation.

"You were the one who brought me here and asked me to do what I could to improve. I have followed your orders, Master, and I've come to realize that I might go far, if I am careful and take time to perfect my act. I was under the impression that this was what you wanted, too." She saw that some of Barantosz's ferocity was fading, and she took advantage of this. "I have an obligation to my family to do all that I can, so that one day we can all be free. They lavished their time and their skills on me, and I want to be worthy of their trust. I never meant to speak against you."

"It's your right to free your family, of course, if you can get the money," Barantosz growled.

"I have enough to buy Macon's freedom right now, but not the rest. One day, when I am too old to ride in the arena, I will buy my own freedom. If you will permit me, Master, to go to Troas, you'll be well rewarded for it. I wish to go as far as my abilities can take me." This was more forthright than was proper for her to be when speaking to the man who owned her, but saying the words gave her satisfaction, and she waited for her master's response with some apprehension.

"What if I took you back. There are many slaves who would be happy to breed with you, and your children might have a better chance than you to free you and the rest of your family. Three children performing make more money than one girl." He nodded to himself. "I'd protect my investment that way, and there would be no risk. If I send you on, there could be . . . well, any number of things to go wrong."

Tishtry felt as if her bones had gone soft inside her, so great was her fear that Barantosz had already made up his mind. "What you do is your decision, Master, and I will abide by it, as I must. But if you decide to breed me, it would mean you would have to wait a long time for the money you want, and during that time, the value of my family would decline through age, and in the end you would not get as much for any of us. If I do well, you could find yourself much richer than you are, and without gambling for years and years on the sort of children I might have." To her own ears she sounded defeated, but apparently Barantosz did not notice.

"You speak boldly for a slave," he chided her.

"I do not mean to offend you."

Barantosz shook his head. "You're a feisty girl, there's no denying that. And you have a mind of your own. That may stand you in good stead in the arena, but it is not the best thing for a slave to be so independent." He paused and chewed his lower lip. "Atadillius believes that you will be very popular wherever you go." He hesitated. "I am minded to give you one year in which to demonstrate your worth. In that time, you will have to earn back all that I have invested in bringing you here, and show me that your value has increased enough to offset the loss of a child, which you would have in a year if I take you home."

This was the first positive thing Tishtry had heard from Barantosz and she seized on it. "You will have better from me letting me perform in the arena than using me for breeding."

"It's likely," Barantosz said with no trace of satisfaction. "A girl like you is not the best for bearing. In a year, you will have enough of a chance to prove your claim, and that is as reasonable as a man can be."

Tishtry nodded. "I will show my worth," she promised, at once pleasantly surprised and terrified. "A year in Troas and other arenae, you will see, I will make my way."

"I will tell your father of this when I reach home." He paused. "You need have no concern for your sister."

"Macon?" The thought of being without her older sister dashed Tishtry's sense of triumph at once. "Are you taking her home?"

"No. She's one less for you to buy now. The Master of the Bestiarii has bought her from me. He says he needs a good saddler here, and that you will need more tack when you go on. He drives a hard bargain, that one." Barantosz shrugged heavily. "This world is not for me. I cannot sort out all the currents that run here. At home, I know what is right and reasonable, but not here."

"Master?" Tishtry blinked. She had always thought Barantosz a dithering fool, but never, until that moment, had she felt sorry for him.

"You seem to do well enough. I'm counting on that, and so is your family. Remember that." He turned away from her, then looked back once. "I hope you do well, girl. I will lose good slaves if you prosper, but . . ." His words trailed away as he started away from her once more. This time he did not look back.

Tishtry stared after him, filled with confusion. Her life, which had seemed so bleak before, now had the promise she had longed for. Yet mixed with this elation was worry; she had said she would prove herself in the year she had been given, but now she had to admit to doubts, and they weighed her down, along with the realization that there was no longer any turning back except in total defeat.

Dozei whickered and nuzzled her neck, as if reminding her that they had work to do. The other three horses caught something of his restlessness.

"Very well," she said aloud, trying to put her turmoil aside in the familiar routine of practice.

Macon was flustered by Tishtry's question, and she did not answer it at once. "He said he needed a saddler. That's what he told Barantosz."

"But that isn't all there is to it, is there?" Tishtry asked. They had finished their evening meal and were sitting by the small brick stove in the corner of the room; unlike the residents of the great villae, they did not have their heat from a central furnace that circulated warm air just under the floor, and so there were few parts of their quarters that were not cold.

"Not all," Macon admitted. "He is fond of me."

"And?" Tishtry pursued. "What more?"

Macon picked up a length of leather and began automatically to work it through her fingers, softening and shining it. "He has said that he will . . . make me his wife."

Tishtry stared. "Wife? But why?"

"For protection. As a freedwoman, I am still part of our family, but as his wife, I am part of his." She shrugged. "And he may simply want to have a wife, like a freeman has."

"But your children would be freemen in any case," Tishtry pointed out. "Never mind. Don't try to explain it to me. If you want to be his wife, that's fine with me. But who would have thought that any of us would be married?" She laughed and stretched out her muscular legs to the warmth. "When will this happen?"

"Sometime in the spring, after we have left for Troas," Macon answered, some of her habitual calm returning. "We will go to the magistrates and record the marriage contract and then have a celebration." She blushed deeply. "A marriage contract. Imagine that."

"And what then? Do you return here or what?" Tishtry felt a pang of loneliness as she said this, because

71

she could sense that although Macon had not gone home with Chimbue Barantosz, she was still leaving her.

"I will do what Atadillius requires of me, I suppose," Macon said, frowning. "He has already given his word that I may continue to make tack of all kinds, and that work and money will be mine, of course, but there are responsibilities to being a wife and he has good reason to expect me to . . . to honor them and him." She looked down at her hands. "He is not a bad man, and I like him. When he tells me stories, I laugh at them because they please me, not because I want to please him."

Tishtry shrugged. "Well, if that is what you want, then you are fortunate to have it. I would rather keep as I am than be paired with a man. Maybe when I am older, I'll change my mind as you have." She rubbed her hands together. "I ought to be grateful, Macon. Atadillius has spared me the task of buying your freedom. But I was looking forward to doing it. If I earn enough to free the rest of our family, I will not be able to see it, but with you here with me, I thought that there would be one time that I could see it, could share in the celebration. And now, that's not possible."

"Tishtry!" Macon said, not quite able to keep the rebuke out of her voice. "How can you begrudge me this?"

"Oh, I don't," Tishtry responded quickly. "I didn't mean it that way. But I wanted to have the opportunity . . ." She faltered, then went on, "I know it's foolish, but I always thought it would be my right to be the one to free you. That is what our father taught me from the first. Don't you understand? I'm glad you are free and that you will have a husband and have children that are freemen and never wear a collar. You will not be paired off with another slave at the master's orders, and need never fear again that it might happen. You're the first of us to be free, Macon. It was something I wanted to give you, for all of us."

Macon sighed and reached out to put her hand on Tishtry's shoulder. "Little sister, you are shaming me."

"No, no," Tishtry protested. "I don't want you to feel shame. I just wanted you to know why . . ."

The sisters looked at each other in silence. Then Macon gave her attention to the stove. "You have enough to contend with, Tishtry. I've thought for some time that it was not proper for our father to expect so much of you."

"*I* don't mind," Tishtry said with a touch of pride.

"Not now. But in a year, you may. Barantosz has only given you a year, and that is not very long. You have too much of a burden now. At least you need not carry me along with the rest." She finished adding wood, then slid the grate back into place.

"But I don't *mind*!" Tishtry insisted. "And if that is why you are going to be Atadillius' wife—"

"No," Macon said. "No. I will be his wife because it is what I want to be. If he had not freed me, but only bought me, he still might have taken me with my goodwill. There are few men I would rather be paired with." Color rose in her face again. "That's the true reason, Tishtry."

"Ah," Tishtry said, trying to sound as if she understood, no matter how baffled she was.

VII

From Apollonia, Tishtry, Macon, and Atadillius took a ship onto the Pontus Euxinus, south and east to Byzantium, then westward through the Propontis, with Thracia on the north of them and Asia and Bithynia on the south. They arrived in Troas four days later, bored and restless from the confinement of the ship, and with the horses suffering from frets and fidgets that made them hard to handle.

At the amphitheater, they were met by the Master of the Bestiarii, a grizzled old Greek with a much-broken nose and an enormous paunch that overhung his belt. He sniffed once at Tishtry's mismatched team and stared hard at Atadillius. "You're the one that fellow Barantosz sent?"

"Yes," Atadillius answered. "I'm Master of the Bestiarii in Apollonia in Thracia." He tried to make it sound important, but in this larger amphitheater, he felt intimidated.

"Huh!" the Greek scoffed, then looked once more at Tishtry. "You're the Armenian, aren't you?"

"Yes," Tishtry answered, aware for the first time that her speech marked her as a complete provincial.

"I've heard about you. Tomorrow I want to see if what they say is true." He braced his hands on his hips and planted his feet apart, as if he expected a struggle.

"The day after would be better. My team has been on a ship for four days and they will need to be worked on the lunge before I yoke them up again." She was pleased to see that this protest had gained her a small measure of respect.

"Day after tomorrow, then," he agreed, and started to walk away.

"Where are we to stay?" Atadillius called after him.

"How should I know? That is Barantosz's concern, not mine. You'll find taverns all around the amphitheater. They'll have room. There are stalls at the end of the stable yard that you can use until we move you to permanent quarters." He waved his hand once, and then was gone.

Macon looked astonished and turned to Atadillius. "What behavior!"

"They're always like this in the big cities," Atadillius lamented, and gave a philosophical hitch to his shoulders. He did not want to admit how little confidence he felt now that he was out of his own amphitheater.

"We'd better get the horses stabled and then find a place to sleep for the night," Tishtry said, paying little attention to either Atadillius or Macon. "I want to see that they get raisins with their grain tonight. It will help them tomorrow." She signaled one of the grooms to assist her, and led her horses toward the far end of the stable yard, as the Greek had told her to do.

"Say there, youngster!" a tall charioteer called as Tishtry made her way toward the stalls. "What's a kitten like you doing with a quadriga?"

She paused, searching for the taunting man. "Driving it in the arena," she answered firmly. "Just like you."

"You race?" The man laughed.

"No, I do other things," she replied, and regretted it as soon as she had said it. There was bawdy laughter from some of the men in the courtyard that angered her.

"What other things, kitten?"

Tishtry turned to him and stared hard at him. "I do tricks. The day after tomorrow, you may judge for yourself what they are worth." With that, she continued toward the stalls, paying no more attention to the comments that followed her.

She stayed on at the stables while her horses were fed and watered, then she made certain that there was a salt lick for each of them, that their coats were brushed and their manes and tails combed free of tangles, before she left the amphitheater and started in the direction of the street of the taverns, where Atadillius and Macon had found lodging. As she walked, she stared about her in wonder, amazed at how crowded, huge, and busy the place was. Everyone seemed to have something to do and was in a hurry to do it. People bustled through the streets, unmindful of those around them, their manners brusque and abrupt.

"They're going to be curious about you," Atadillius promised Tishtry when she reached the tavern. "I heard some of the aurigatores talking about you, saying that they had heard you were skilled. Most of them expected one of those strapping great women, like the Cimri have, not a compact thing like you." He held out a plate of fish chunks cooked with grapes. "Better have some."

Tishtry helped herself, looking at her sister. "I want to go over the tack tonight, just in case we need to make any repairs."

Macon looked down at her fingers. "If you think it's best."

"Of course it's best. No one performs when there's something wrong with her equipment." She ate some more, thinking that she had become hungry during her walk. "Do they have any nuts? I'm famished for nuts."

"Probably they have almonds in the kitchen. They have sausages, too. Do you want them?" Atadillus was being kinder than usual, but Tishtry did not question his reasons.

"Fine. If I'm going to do a demonstration ride, I might as well have as much energy as I can get." She leaned back on her stool, bracing precariously on one leg. "Who knows, someday we may eat lying down like all the high-ranking Romans do. Wouldn't that be a treat."

"Tishtry!" Macon chided her. "Remember where we are and that we are guests in this city."

Tishtry shrugged. "I'll be respectful, if that's what's needed. But I won't take time to cater to those charioteers at the arena—they all think that I'm incapable of riding decently because I'm young and I'm short.''

"You'll have to show them otherwise, won't you?'' Atadillius said, winking at Macon. "They'll find out.''

"They will,'' Tishtry promised.

"I'd do better if I had another horse,'' Tishtry complained to Atadillius two days later. "They want me to ride again, and with Shirdas favoring his off rear hoof, I can't do it. If I had another horse, to take over when one of mine is not well, then I would be able to do far more than I'm doing now.''

"Ask Barantosz,'' Atadillius suggested. They were at the practice ring near the arena and Tishtry was taking a break from her morning exercise with her team.

"He'll say no. He's already irritated at how much all this is costing, and how little he has had to show for it so far.'' She folded her arms and looked across the ring to where an African bestiarii was working with a horse and a lion, teaching the half-grown cat to ride on the horse's back. "I wish I could do something like that. Look at him; those animals are marvelous, and everyone will remember him forever because of how well he does this.''

"They'll remember you, too, Tishtry,'' Atadillius assured her, smiling at her with more friendship than he usually showed her.

"Possibly,'' she said without a trace of vanity. "And possibly not. If I could do something truly spectacular—''

"You already do spectacular things,'' Atadillius reminded her.

"Not *truly* spectacular. I wish I had something more to my performance, a trick or series of tricks that no one would be able to duplicate in a hundred years." She reached out and patted Shirdas' neck. "He'll be better in a day or two and then he'll have a chance to show them all what he can do. That will still those ugly whispers."

"What whispers?" Atadillius wanted to know.

"They're saying that most of what I do is sham and that my master is trying to hoax everyone, creating interest in a charioteer as a novelty and then delivering nothing." She turned to glare at Atadillius. "I'm not going to let them say that. I won't have it."

Atadillius decided that he should not encourage her in her attitude, for it might lead to more difficulties than she was already having. "You will show them to everyone's satisfaction. There is no use in telling them, for they are used to hearing idle boasts. Be patient, girl, and you will have your chance. After that, they may say what they will, you will have no cause to concern yourself with them."

"Perhaps," she allowed, her expression set in stubborn lines. "But it is maddening to know that they doubt my abilities."

"They will not in a day or so," he soothed.

Tishtry patted her horses once more. "I've been working on another running mount. I think I'll try it out when I have my first demonstration. It looks far more dangerous than it is, but I don't mind that."

"How do you mean?" Atadillius asked, trying to hide his worry, for he knew that Macon relied on him to keep Tishtry from attempting anything reckless.

"Well, I worked it out yesterday, and I tried it out with Immit. I'd show you now, but with that lion in the ring, I don't think Immit would manage well. What I do is start the team going, then jump out of the quadriga. I let the team go on, run across the arena so that I meet them as they come out of the turn, I spring back into the quadriga, then up, onto Immit. It's really quite easy, if they keep to a steady pace."

Atadillius gulped. "You might be trampled if you mistimed your . . . spring."

"Oh, I'm not afraid of that," she said blithely, unaware of the distress she was causing Atadillius. "The team is used to me and they'll stop quickly if I falter."

"You could still be dragged for quite a distance," he pointed out.

"It's unlikely. I'd be more apt to roll free, the way I was taught to do. My father taught me about rolling away before he ever put me on a horse." She reached up for the reins. "I'd better get back to work. This is no time to be lazy."

"Is the fifth horse so important," Atadillius asked, anticipating her answer.

"I wouldn't have said it if it wasn't so," she answered as she led her horses back into the ring for more work.

Her stage fright had returned, but she was used to it, and it did not upset her as it had the first time. She took a few long, deep breaths, then nodded to the aurigatore, bringing her head up and smiling widely. The glare from the sun and the sand hurt her eyes, but she kept the smile as she blinked.

There was the roar she had come to expect, but this one was louder and it echoed in a way she had never heard before. She was glad that the brass studs on her tunica and breeches had been polished, because, in so large an arena, she was worried she would not easily be seen. Tishtry swung by the editor's box and gave the customary bow before vaulting into the air, turning a somersault, and landing on Amath's back. She could tell from the sound that this had been a success. She let her horses make a circuit of the arena while she simply stood on Amath's back.

On the second turn, she started her tricks, and had the satisfaction of hearing gasps and hoots from the crowd as she rose on one leg on Immit's back. She flashed her grin at the editor's box again and continued around the arena. She liked the larger amphitheater now that she was used to it, for it gave her more room to show off. She turned a somersault between horses and came up on Dozei, letting the sorrel's mane blow in her face before she got to her feet. Next she steadied herself, then tried the most difficult of her tricks: standing on her hands on Shirdas' back. She was only able to hold herself erect for a little distance, but she could tell she had her triumph in that trick by the enthusiasm of the audience. She ran through the rest of her stunts quickly, then exited through the Gates of Life at the far end of the arena, beaming to herself.

"That was some display," one of the Greek chari-oteers said as he came up to her. "You're better than I thought you'd be."

"My master expects it of me," she answered, determined not to be falsely modest, but not to puff herself up, either. "He's sent me here because he thinks I'll do well for him."

"If that performance was any indication of your skill, I'd say he has every reason to be confident of you." It was a gallant compliment, but said with a trace of mockery that infuriated Tishtry.

"How kind you are," she said through her teeth, then turned to accept the praise of several other arena performers, trying not to let the Greek's snide attitude spoil her sense of accomplishment.

"Your horses are quite surprising," one of the bestiarii told her as she walked her team to cool them. "To look at them, you'd think they'd never pull as one, but when they're in the arena, they're better than most of the racing teams."

"I chose them for that," Tishtry said with excusable pride. "They have the same length of stride and Shirdas here is strong enough to hold the others in the turns." She looked toward the Gates of Life. "I heard there was to be a venation. What are they hunting?"

"There are eight dwarfs hunting wild pigs. I've seen better contests, but not in as backward a place as this. Troas is a disappointing place." He gestured philosophically. "Well, when you reach my age, what can you expect? I'm too old for working in the important amphitheaters."

Tishtry was amazed to hear him speak so, for she still thought of this amphitheater as the most impressive she had ever seen. "If this is poor, what are the great ones like?"

The old bestiarii laughed. "Why, child, they are gigantic, with ten times the number of seats you have here, and the Games last for two and three days, with hundreds of animals, some of them brought from the farthest ends of the Empire. There are four and five chariot races, and the performers have skills that you cannot imagine. In Roma once, I saw a team of Dacian boys trained to swim as a team, and they pulled a barge through the flooded arena performing great and beautiful movements as fine as any dance. They then fought a mock battle with a miniature bireme manned by monkeys. After that, three of the boys performed with dolphins. Then they had a true battle with sharks. A number of them were killed, but not as many as you might expect. They are very expert, those Daci. The crowd loved them."

It was more than Tishtry could picture. "How do they flood the arena?" she asked, thinking of what seemed the most impossible.

"There are special seals at both the Gates of Life and the Gates of Death, and there are pipes that lead from the aqueduct to the amphitheater. They've had to raise the stands and the spina because of it, but no one minds." He had a faraway look in his eyes and he spoke slowly, dreamily.

"I cannot think how it would be possible," she said, shaking her head.

"Wait until you see it for yourself," the bestiarii said, patting her arm in a friendly way.

"I hope I will." Now it was Tishtry's turn to have her thoughts go a great distance from where she was.

"Oh, I have no doubt you will," he said, cheering her with his offhanded attitude. "If you keep on as you've started, they'll be wild for you in Roma."

Tishtry cocked her head to the side. "I hope you are right."

He chuckled. "Do you want to be the talk of Roma?"

She turned to him in surprise. "Of course. Then I would be able to buy my family's freedom and set money aside for when I can no longer perform with my team. When that happens, I will buy my own freedom and find a place where I can breed horses."

The old bestiarii shook his head in astonishment. "You're either a very clearheaded girl, or you have been trained by an extremely sensible man. In either case, count yourself fortunate, for there are those who can think of nothing beyond the next adventure on the sands. They are the ones who take the needless risks and end up going out the Gates of Death."

"My father trained me," Tishtry said, not quite as cordially as before. As always, a compliment made her suspicious.

"Then he knew what he was about. You should be grateful," the old bestiarii said to her. He gave her an offhanded salute and left her to her chores with her team.

CHAPTER

VIII

Tishtry was bent over Amath's rear hoof, examining it for chips and splits, when she heard someone speak her name. Startled, she straightened up, releasing the bay's leg as she did. "Yes?" She glanced out of the stall to see who had addressed her.

"You are Tishtry, the Armenian charioteer?" the man said, his regular features giving no hint of his emotions. He wore a linen dalmatica belted with gold, and there was a signet ring on his middle finger. His brown hair had been curled, and he smelled faintly of lilac and nutmeg.

"Yes." She made a gesture of respect, wondering as she did so why a high-ranking Roman would wish to have words with her.

"I am Gnaeus Calpurnius," he said, as if this should mean something to her.

"It is an honor to speak with you, sir," she responded

in as gracious a manner as she knew, though she was still puzzled.

"I've seen you work, both in the ring and in the arena. You're very good." He smiled at her. "I've seen many charioteers and stunt riders in my day, and you promise to be one of the best ever."

She thought he had chosen a strange way to compliment her, and was afraid that he might be trying to offer her a bribe, but she held her tongue. Her command of Latin was not terribly good, and she was afraid she might misinterpret what he said and offend him. "It is a pleasure to hear you say this."

"And no doubt in time you will be even better than you are now," he went on. "It will require a guide who is knowledgeable in the ways of the Games, and someone with the associates who appreciate talent like yours."

"My master has invested much in me," Tishtry said, frowning now.

"No doubt, no doubt," Calpurnius said in an apologetic manner. "But he is not a Roman, or so I have been told, and although he raises fine horses for the Legions and the arena, he is not a man with much experience of the Games, which might be to your disadvantage."

"What are you saying, good Roman?" Tishtry asked sharply.

Calpurnius did not answer her directly. "You can see why it is that I am concerned for you. It would distress me to see ability like yours languish in the provinces because your master has not the funds or the connections to advance you properly."

"It is improper for me to listen to this," Tishtry reminded him. "No slave should hear her master abused."

"But I am not abusing him," Calpurnius protested. "He has done a very fine job for you, given the limits of his resources. But there are those who would be able to do so much more than he has done. It is my intention to offer to buy you; have you any objections?"

This announcement made Tishtry blink. "Buy me?" she repeated, shocked.

"Surely you've been thinking of it? Wouldn't another master serve your ambitions better than the Armenian who owns you?" He waited, and when she said nothing, continued. "If I am the first to suggest this, then I am astonished, for a charioteer of your abilities must attract all sorts of attention. But if there is some reason why it would not be possible for you to call me master, I would like to know of it."

Tishtry found her mouth suddenly very dry. "I want to buy my family's freedom."

"You can do that more swiftly with me than with Barantosz. He does not have the opportunities that I can give you." He had a disarming smile, one that showed his lined face kindly.

"He might not consent," Tishtry warned.

"Let me speak with him, and we'll see what comes of it. You may be right, and he will not agree, or will set the price so high that no one will want to bargain with him." He smoothed his dalmatica. "As long as you would not mind the change, I will approach him."

Tishtry came a few steps nearer. "Why do you ask me? You may purchase me and be done with it."

"So I might," Calpurnius said candidly. "And I might then find myself with an expensive and unwilling slave on my hands, one with abilities that she could refuse to use to their fullest. You could decide that your horses could not manage the change, or that one of them was in danger of foundering. Believe me, all these things have happened to slave owners at one time or another. I would prefer not to have such troubles."

Tishtry could not help smiling. "Yes, that could happen, but I would not behave so shabbily. My father told me long ago that it is important for a slave to show value to his master."

"Very wise, your father," Calpurnius said. "You own four horses, your tack, and your quadriga. What else?"

"Very little. My clothes and my copper bracelets, a satchel to carry my things while traveling, two pairs of Persian boots, a few personal goods, that is about the sum of it. I would like to have another horse, so that if one of the team suffers, I need not stop appearing while the horse recovers." She felt very worldly now, and decided that she would be able to do more with her life than she had thought a year ago. "I would want to perform in other amphitheaters, if that is not inconvenient."

"I hope you will. It would be in both our interests to have that happen." He nodded to her. "Are we striking a bargain?"

"Slaves cannot bargain," she reminded him primly. "But it would not distress me to call you master." It was improper to admit so much, but she could not deny her enthusiasm.

"Very good. Be as circumspect when you are mine and I will see that you are handsomely rewarded. Oh," he added in a different tone, "I will deal harshly with you if you take bribes."

Tishtry drew herself erect, feeling very angry. "I would not dishonor my family or my master. I may not speak smoothly or have high-bred manners, but I know what I owe my master, and you may be sure I will conduct myself properly." She did not like his implication, and wished she had better ways to tell him so.

Calpurnius chuckled. "And a firebrand as well. There, don't bristle at me that way, my girl. I have no doubt you'll behave well." Again he smiled at her, and she felt her anger evaporate.

"You should not have said that to me." It would be more correct to apologize, but she could not quite bring herself to do that. She wished she could find out if the man was as serious as he claimed to be, or if he was only amusing himself by asking her these questions. The man was a Roman, and wealthy enough to wear gold. His accent was educated and his manners were beautiful. What sort of master would he be? She wished she could ask him what other arena slaves he owned, so that she could find out from them what they thought of him.

He gave her a measuring look. "Take care, girl, for you could make enemies with that ready tongue of yours. There are those who would not be as forgiving as I am, especially of a barbarian slave." His wave was lazy and good-natured as he turned away from the stall. "I will speak to you again soon, after I have had a word or two with your owner."

"All right," she replied, and tried to concentrate again

on Amath's hooves. It took all of her willpower to keep to her task, for her curiosity was burning in her, though there was no way to answer the questions that plagued her.

"So you have a Roman tribune wanting to buy you," Atadillius said to Tishtry a few days later.

"I think there is a Roman who *says* he wants to buy me," Tishtry corrected, knowing that it was wise to be cautious in these dealings.

"He's written to Barantosz; that's a good indication of how serious his intentions are." He folded his arms and looked down at her, eyes narrowed. "I cannot make up my mind—you are either the innocent you appear to be, or you are sly beyond your years. Which is it?"

"I can't answer a question like that," Tishtry said, determined not to be insulted. "You shame me even to ask."

"Don't take that tone with me," Atadillius ordered. "You are going beyond what is proper in a slave."

Now Tishtry was stung. "You have not called me a slave before!"

"You haven't made it necessary," Atadillius told her severely. "Look here, Tishtry: you have come a little way, and you think that now you are one with the great charioteers. You're in error, girl. The great ones are so far above you that you would seem little more than an apprentice to them, which is what you are. Don't forget who brought you to this point, and I'll have no more of your insolence."

Tishtry was deeply shocked by Atadillius' outburst. "Why do you accuse me? What have I done?"

"You're forgetting who you are and where you come from," Atadillius warned her. "You are thinking beyond yourself."

With real insight, Tishtry shook her head. "No, Atadillius. You are afraid that I will advance beyond you, and you will then have to return to your own amphitheater and have no chance to go to Roma." Over his sputtered and indignant protests, she went on, "You believe that I will carry you where you want to go. You see yourself being Master of the Bestiarii in a larger amphitheater than Apollonia, and you intend that I should make you that."

"You *have* got beyond yourself," Atadillius blustered.

"No, but perhaps I have got beyond you. We'll see." She took a few steps back. "I am sorry to speak to you this way because of my sister, but if Macon knew of this, she would be very much shocked."

"One Roman makes a few vague suggestions and you start imagining yourself as the most celebrated charioteer in the Empire!" he scoffed.

Her eyes were somber. "You know that isn't so. You must not say such things, or it will be more difficult for me with the others. Already they resent me because of what I can do, and if you start speaking against me, they will assume they can do much to annoy me, and that would be a misfortune for all of us. Including you, Atadillius."

"You're being a fool," he warned her, but would say no more, choosing to sit far away from her, making a point of ignoring her while she rubbed her saddles and harness with wax.

———

Barantosz sent his reply by messenger, and Atadillius read it with pleasure. "You are not going to be sold to anyone, Tishtry," he informed her that evening as they gathered for supper in the tavern where they had lodging. "You are going to stay his slave at least for a year. So curb those ambitions of yours and be glad that I did not take your outbursts too seriously."

"It is not for me to say who will own me," Tishtry answered with a shrug, but with inner surprise as she realized that she was disappointed that Barantosz had not accepted the offer of Gnaeus Calpurnius. "It is not fitting for me to consider one master over another."

"So long as you remember that," Atadillius said smugly, then turned toward Macon. "We are going to be sent on to Salonae. Barantosz wishes to see how she does in a slightly larger amphitheater."

"Salonae?" Tishtry said, puzzled at her master's order.

"When are we to leave?" Macon asked at the same time.

"In Salonae there are longer Games, and you will have to compete with some truly capable charioteers and stunt riders, not like here where you are something of a novelty and have got a following on the strength of it." Atadillius nodded with satisfaction. "Consider how it has been for you so far, and realize that now you will be required to show something more than three or four tricks if you are to be worth anything."

"Atadillius, for the gods' sake," Macon protested.

"It is for her own good that I say this, Macon. You're Tishtry's sister, and you can't see how she's been changing. She's too taken with herself, and she supposes that she's more important than she is. Her master's made sure that she won't be so foolish in future, and will justify his time and attention with learning her craft in a fitting manner. She's been too much indulged, and he's been so lenient that she's supposed it was her right to behave with unfitting pride."

"That's not true!" Tishtry insisted. "And you haven't suffered. Anytime you've arranged for me to appear, you've earned your sweetening, just as I've earned mine. You don't want to lose that, do you?"

Atadillius sneered. "You haven't been careful in your behavior, and now you're upset because you're not permitted to continue as you've been going." He paused, his eyes full of false pity. "I can tell you're cast down, and that's not surprising. You've had too much adulation too young, and you don't yet know what the world is like. You believe that because the people here praise you, you will meet the same endorsement everywhere. Barantosz is wise enough to know that this isn't true, and he's chosen to show you your error now, while only a reprimand is required rather than chastisement. You ought to be grateful."

"You're sorry to lose the money," Tishtry repeated. "You've enjoyed all the attention as much as I have." She shook her head. "For Macon's sake, I don't want to fight with you, Atadillius, but if I've let the approval of the crowd go to my head, you've let your power and influence go to yours."

"*I* didn't make up my mind to take you to task; Barantosz did," he said, his features flushing.

Tishtry tossed her head. "Chimbue Barantosz never had such a thought in his life; he's too indecisive for that. If he thinks ill of me, it's because someone has persuaded him that I'm behaving badly.'' She stared at Atadillius. ''Who would that person be, do you think?''

''You're being foolish,'' Atadillius said, but his face darkened and he refused to meet her eyes. ''Besides, it is for your own good.''

''No; for your good,'' Tishtry countered. ''You have done well for yourself being the one who manages me, and no one has challenged your right to all you have said and done, which has been sufficient until now. You know that it's not so any longer, and you are afraid that you will lose whatever advantage I have provided you if I compete in larger amphitheaters or have another, more ambitious master. You know this is true, Atadillius.'' She paused to gather her thoughts. ''You helped me very much, and you have freed my sister, and for those two things alone, I am grateful to you, and always will be. Yet I cannot hold myself back for you, or protect you.''

''Protect me?'' he jeered.

''You want to advance yourself, and that is wise of you. But you intend to use me for that advance, and I won't let you. It would not be correct for you or for me.'' She got up. ''I'm sorry, Macon. I have to go see to my team, and then I will stay in the stables tonight.''

Macon, confused and worried by all she had heard, made no objection to this. She turned her large eyes up toward Atadillius. ''You are being harsh, my master.''

''I am being sensible,'' he informed her. Then, looking hard at Tishtry, he shook his head. ''Very well. If you must make this fruitless gesture, go ahead. Sleep with your horses and share their vermin."

Tishtry laughed at this, which made Atadillius stand more straight than ever. "What's a flea or two? There are plenty of them in this tavern, and I'm used to them. The rats stay away from me for the most part, and I haven't found a scorpion yet." She cocked her head to the side. "Do you think I should be on guard against them, Atadillius?"

"There are very few scorpions in the stable," he grumbled.

"Then I will not look out for them too much," Tishtry said, reaching for her short cloak, cut like the caracalla that soldiers wore.

"I'd like you to eat with us in the morning," Macon ventured, not looking at either her sister or the man who now owned her.

"If there's time. I have to exercise the team and go over the quadriga. I want to try some new tricks with it." She wanted, too, a chance to be alone, so that she could sort out her feelings.

"More tricks to impress the Roman?" Atadillius suggested in a snide tone. "You want to convince him you're worth the price that Barantosz will ask, is that it?"

"No, I want to impress the crowds I perform for," Tishtry responded hotly. "I am obligated to them, even more than to my master, no matter who owns me. My worth is determined by the crowd. As you yourself taught me. What the crowd likes makes my success. You have bought Macon, but there are others still depending on me to earn their freedom." She tossed the folded cloak over her shoulder. "I'm sorry you over-heard all this, Macon. It's not pleasant for you, just as it isn't pleasant for me."

"Then you should listen to my good advice," Atad-illius could not resist saying to Tishtry. "You're too headstrong."

"When I hear good advice, I listen," Tishtry told him, and went for the door. "I suppose you mean well, Atad-illius. I hope you mean well. But you're wrong."

She was still very angry, but had tried to hold herself in check. Now that she was away from the aggravation of Atadillius, she had to admit that she had been hoping that one of the Romans would buy her and let her perform in larger, more important amphitheaters. When she was in the arena, she knew that she was capable of the most unusual performances. She had to be better, she knew that, and for that she would need more op-portunity than she had been given so far. There was no doubt in her mind that Barantosz would not want her to advance any further. He was making good money on her now and there was very little risk. Perhaps the same was true of Atadillius, who could always get her a place in any Games here for a good fee, but would not have that certainty at another amphitheater. She sighed as she walked, going to the charioteers' entrance to the amphitheater.

"Staying with your team, are you?" the scarred old slave who kept the door asked as he recognized Tishtry.

"I ought to. Immit has been fractious lately and needs attention." She smiled at the old slave as he opened the gate to her.

"Strange team you have," he said. "What possessed you to train such dissimilar horses?"

By now Tishtry had grown tired of answering the question, and of justifying her choice to the superstitious who thought that mismatched teams were unlucky. "Only their coats are dissimilar," Tishtry pointed out in patient annoyance. "Their strides match perfectly."

The old man shook his head, laughing a bit. "You youngsters: always trying something new and outrageous."

"It's expected of us," Tishtry said lightly, swaggering a little as she walked away toward the stables.

CHAPTER

IX

Within the month another letter came from Chimbue Barantosz, saying that he had decided that Tishtry was ready for more advancement; he would send one of his older charioteers to her to accompany her to Salonae, where she would perform in the arena. They were to depart within seven days of the old charioteer's arrival and would remain until he ordered her back, or to another amphitheater.

Atadillius was nonplussed at this development. "I am astounded that your master could want this" was all he could say, and he repeated it several times, as if he would come to understand Barantosz's decision better if he said the words enough.

"I understand that he has had reports from others who attend the Games, and they have advised him to send me on," Tishtry said carefully. She had done her best to keep their arguments to a minimum for Macon's sake.

"I will have to send a message to him, explaining that you are not prepared."

Tishtry joined her hands together and studied her fingers. "You would return to Apollonia, wouldn't you, if my master sent me on?"

"Of course," he said with more bluster than he had intended.

"And Macon would go with you," Tishtry said, more softly.

"She is mine now, and I would want her with me." He stopped abruptly. "You would miss her, wouldn't you?"

"Yes; I miss all the others, too," she admitted. She had been rubbing wax into her boots to make them shine, but she stopped to look squarely at Atadillius. "Once she is gone, I will probably never see any of them again. That is a slave's lot. When they are free, they will have to make their way in the world, as I will have to do, when my days on the sands are over. Then it might be possible to find them all again, but . . ." She picked up her boot and went back to work on it with renewed determination.

"You're what, fifteen years old?" Atadillius asked.

"Almost." She put the right boot aside and picked up the left one.

"It could be many years before you are free."

"It could be never." She sighed. "I have much to learn. You think I do not know this, but you're in error. I know that there are many things I have to correct in what I do, and improvements I must master. But I will do it, Atadillius. I know I will do it."

Atadillius shrugged. "You will not listen to me, and

so I suppose you must learn your limitations for your-self."

"Yes, I must." She looked at her boots, examining them critically. "You have done as you think best and in the manner you think best. What I hope now is that you will care for Macon. She is a woman who is gentle and kind, and there are times she is more distressed because of it." She got off the bench and picked up her boots. "It would have been better if my master had permitted me another horse. I must abide by his decision, but I fret when one of my horses is not in top form. It is a risk to the horse and to me."

"I will inform him of that," Atadillius said stiffly.

"You need not. If he will not believe me, it will take more than you or his charioteer to persuade him." She padded across the rough planking to where her small leather chest stood open. "Macon is binding all the traces for me so that they will be tougher and last longer. She is a good sister."

"You have said so before," Atadillius remarked.

"I could say it every hour and it would not be the whole of it." Tishtry put her boots into the chest, then pulled out a pair of sandals, which she set on the floor. Bending over at the waist, she began to loosen the laces. "If there is a scribe you can use, ask Macon to send me word when she can. I will find someone to read it to me."

"I will." He paused while she put on her sandals. "We have had harsh words, Tishtry."

"They were not what I would want," she said as she tied the last knot.

100

"You made accusations." He sounded petulant, and he waited for her to respond.

"I said what I thought was so. That hasn't changed, Atadillius. I have never said you did anything for malice, but you are a man who defends his own advantage. There is nothing wrong with that, unless your advantage is not also my advantage." She stood up, her features flushed.

"It was not only for my advantage," he insisted. "I believe that you are not yet ready for the challenges you seem so eager to accept."

"I may never be ready for them," Tishtry said candidly. "But I will not know until I try, will I?" She looked at Atadillius, her expression polite and faintly curious, giving him time to answer her.

"You'd better go exercise your team. You have to perform tomorrow." He indicated the door. "The charioteer will be here in a few days. You should be prepared for him."

"I will," she assured him, closing the door as she went out.

The charioteer was a Persian called Naius, a grizzled man nearing forty, with weathered features, a tough, stringy, sun-baked body, and the first signs of the disease of the crab on his shoulder. He regarded Tishtry through bleary eyes and spat in the dust. "So you're the one they're all talking about," he said by way of introduction.

"I'm Tishtry," she said, knowing no other way to respond to this opening.

"Well, the master's certain you're going to bring him a fortune in Salonae. Or so he tells me." He clapped his hands together. "The passage is all arranged. I hear your team and rig are ready. Is there anything else you need to tend to? Better settle up your debts if the master won't cover them for you."

"There's only my keep, and that's paid for. I don't gamble." She was aware that most charioteers were avid bettors, seeking any excuse to make a wager, but so far gambling was not attractive to her.

"Strange," he said. "But you're young enough to have got into little trouble yet. Wait a year or two, when the money's greater and they offer you big bribes and other enticements. I know what it'll be like. There was a time when I did it all myself." He signaled to two of the porters near the tavern. "Bring her chest. There's a ship waiting for us that goes with the tide."

The porters hurried to obey while Tishtry said, "The horses are ready at the amphitheater. One of them is difficult to get onto a ship—Dozei doesn't like ships."

"The men know how to handle that. This is a crew that's brought leopards and crocodiles to arenae all over the Empire. A horse is nothing to them." He inspected Tishtry again. "I heard your sister left yesterday, with her new master."

"She did," Tishtry said, her throat tightening. "We didn't get to say any true farewells."

"It's better if you don't. The parting's less painful that way. You think that it would be otherwise, but it's not. I remember when I was parted from my woman and our two children—I wanted to spend days and days with them, but my master did the wise thing and sent them away without warning. One day I went back to our quarters and they were gone. The grief was over sooner. That's why the Romans have the custom. It's wise of them."

"But I—" She stopped, afraid she would cry.

The old charioteer gave her a rough pat on the shoulder. "I don't mind if you want to weep for her. We may be slaves, but we're still human."

"They didn't have to go like that. There were things I wanted to say." Tishtry swallowed hard and looked away, her lips pressed tightly together.

"Our master said that she's good with tack. You must be sorry to have her gone." He looked at the tavern door, impatient for the porters.

"I will miss her very much," Tishtry said softly.

Naius turned back to her. "There. Don't take it to heart. It's the way of slaves to lose their families. You were fortunate to be with yours for so long." He cleared his throat. "Do they have decent wine at this place?"

"I think so," she answered, irritated by his attitude.

"The crab is eating me," he said matter-of-factly. "There are times I like to drown it in wine. It helps for a while."

Tishtry felt alarmed at this revelation, for she knew what men were like who took to comforting themselves with wine. "Will it be wise, going aboard a ship as we are?"

He laughed roughly. "Why, I've had enough wine in my skin that I don't think it could bother me if we were caught by both Scylla and Charybdis." He grinned at the prospect of this double disaster. "We stop at Apollonia—"

"Apollonia?" Tishtry repeated with amazement.

"Oh, not the one you're thinking of, on the Pontus Euxinus; this one is on our way to Salonae, on the Mare Adriaticum. I raced there when I was much younger. I've seen them all, even the Circus Maximus in Roma. It's an enormous place." He could not conceal the satisfaction he felt. "It will be a pleasant thing to see some of it again. Barantosz lives at the back of the world, though he doesn't know it. Ah! There're the porters. Over here, you sluggards. And bring me two skins of wine while you're at it." He threw them three copper coins, then turned back to Tishtry. "Do you need help carrying this to the boat, or can you manage?"

"I can manage," Tishtry said, more irritated than ever.

"Just as well. No saying what a porter'll do with a chest." He peered up at the sky, watching the clouds. "We might have some rough weather if the wind picks up. How are your horses in a storm?"

Tishtry could not keep her worry out of her voice. "Do you think it will be bad weather? My team . . . I don't want anything to happen to them."

"The captain knows his business, and he isn't about to lose good animals if he can help it. For one thing, he'd have to pay Barantosz for the loss, and that could get expensive."

"To say nothing of the time it would take me to train another horse," Tishtry snapped. "If there is any doubt, it would be best to wait."

"You're being too cautious," he said bluntly. "You're still new to this; give yourself a few years and you'll change your tune—trust me." Naius winked raffishly.

"By the time you're an old hand like me, you'll think nothing of setting out in a gale."

"Not with my team," she declared.

"Get your chest, girl," Naius ordered, closing the argument. "We must be under way."

By the time they reached the dock, the clouds had thickened overhead and the wind was brisk, coming in from the southwest. The transport ship, still tied up, rolled ominously and the gangplank shifted treacherously as Tishtry attempted to help two of the ship's slaves lead Shirdas aboard.

The chestnut rolled his eyes and stamped nervously, squealing as the gangplank rocked. He tried to buck, but was restrained expertly by the ship's slaves on either side of him.

"Don't hurt him. He's got a soft mouth!" Tishtry called to them.

"We know how to do this," the older of the slaves replied, keeping a firm hold on Shirdas' bridle. "We'll have him aboard and in his sling in no time."

Tishtry scowled as she watched them, fearing that at any instant Shirdas would buck and break free, hurting himself and perhaps one of the slaves as well. She did not want to have to get him out of the water, for she could not swim. "Careful!" she shouted as the slaves finally got him onto the deck. "Don't force him; he gets frightened."

This time the slaves did not answer her, being fully occupied with getting Shirdas down the ramp to the stalls belowdecks.

Immit was more cooperative, though she whinnied

in distress at the movement of the ship. The slaves patted her and cajoled her, luring her down into the hold with a nosebag of mixed grains.

When Amath was brought onto the deck, his ears went flat back and he started to rear, his front hooves striking out. Tishtry, still on the dock with Dozei, started to rush onto the ship, but was warned back by Naius.

"You let them handle him. That bay of yours won't be any calmer if you go running up to him in a panic." He spat again. "Drosos is a good captain, and his slaves are the best. They won't bring him to any harm."

"But look at him!" Tishtry protested.

"They'll handle him," Naius repeated. "You look after this sorrel of yours, that's what you need to do."

Reluctantly, Tishtry turned to pat Dozei's neck and blow into his nostrils, trying to reassure him. "You're going to be fine, boy," she said uncertainly as he whickered.

At last the slaves brought Amath under control and had him mincing down the ramp into the hold.

"There, you see? Nothing to it. Why, these slaves could load lions and tigers and ostriches without any problems. You can be sure that horses are nothing to them. They've even carried a rhinoceros once; I heard all about it from Drosos this morning. Tricksy animals, rhinos, and they weigh more than your horses do, too." He rubbed at the discoloration on his shoulder. "Take care that you do not find the crab growing on you, girl. Make sure you wear your tunica all the time you race."

"I wear a leather tunica when I race," she told him, her attention on the ship, not on his warning.

"See that you do." He nodded to the slaves who now emerged from the hold to lead Dozei aboard. "How many other horses do you have aboard this trip?"

"Twelve more than these," the younger one answered. "Two mares in foal among them." He reached out for Dozei's bridle. "Come on, fellow. Your friends are waiting for you." He held out his hand, offering raisins to the sorrel. "Come on," he coaxed.

Naius had tapped the first of his wineskins and took this opportunity to have another drink from it. "Bring your chest aboard, girl. It's time we joined your team."

Dozei did a jittery prance down the ramp, balking only once, when the ship rolled and creaked loudly. The slaves quieted him before taking him all the way below the deck.

"In good weather, they sometimes keep animals on the deck in cages. Not the horses, of course. They can kick the sides out of the cages." Naius gathered up his wineskins and a satchel of belongings and led the way onto the ship. "We have quarters in the front of the vessel, just behind the prow. One bunk each, and we share space with the crew."

"Fine," Tishtry said absently. "Will they permit me to see my team before we cast off?"

"Permit you? They require it. Drosos doesn't want to be accused of negligence when we reach Salonae." He indicated the ladder that led to the slaves' tiny cabin. "Down you go. Leave your chest and then we'll look at your team."

With apprehension, Tishtry climbed down the ladder, fearing as she went that she would miss her footing and fall. It was awkward to hold her chest, for it left her only one hand free to brace herself. "It's dark in here," she complained, disliking not the dark but the smallness of the cabin.

"Then stay on the deck, if it bothers you. There's no reason for you to be here when you're not asleep. You can go back into the hold with your horses, if you like. They're bringing your quadriga aboard now," he added, looking along the deck as he started down the ladder. "Are you going to offer libations to Neptune and Mercury?"

Tishtry paused in the middle of selecting a bunk. "Is it wise?"

"Well, Neptune is god of the sea and of horses, and Mercury protects travelers. Toss a cup of wine overboard to them, when Drosos does, just in case." He offered her his opened wineskin.

"Do you think it makes a difference?" she asked, frowning.

Naius shrugged. "Who knows? I think the crew believes it makes a difference, and that is important, you'll agree."

"Then it should be done," she said, knowing that her master would be offended if his slaves did not observe the customs of the ship. She put her chest on the uppermost bunk, then went back to the ladder, eager to be out of the confined quarters.

On deck, the crew was stowing crates on deck, securing them in place with heavy webbing, while, in the bow, others were loosening the lines to the square sail that hung from the sprit that angled up from the deck. Two men were climbing aft to the high rear deck where the steering oars were located. On the tall mast amidships, slaves were climbing to the spar to let down the large, square sail. The captain stood under the mainmast, shouting instructions to his crew.

"We're ready to make the offering," Naius said when Drosos had paused in his shouting.

"In good time," he said, giving a swift glance their way. "We're about to cast off." He looked up the mast and, apparently satisfied, gave his attention once more to Naius and Tishtry. "So you're the charioteer they're all talking about," he said to her. "I've heard about your tricks."

"I'm honored," Tishtry responded, as was proper.

"You're a credit to your master," Drosos told her, then marched back toward the steering oars, where the guardian image of the ship stood. "We're under the protection of Demeter; Ceres, the Romans call her. She's been good to us so far." He indicated the wooden figure of a young woman holding a sheaf of wheat and barley in her arms. "We started out carrying grain, but there's more money in animals."

Tishtry and Naius followed after him, walking less steadily than the captain, who was used to the rocking motion of his ship. "Do we offer to her as well?" Tishtry asked Naius.

It was Drosos who answered. "Yes." He reached the statue and patted it affectionately. "She's good to merchants." Then he bent and took a flask of wine from beside the statue, opened it, and smeared a little of the wine on the wooden foot of the figure. "Take care of us, my pretty, and we'll get you a new paint job next time we have a layover in Athenae." Then he went to the rail and poured more wine over the side. "Neptune,

109

be kind to us." He poured a second libation. "Mercury, speed us, and without any of your tricks."

Naius opened the neck of his wineskin and poured some of the dark liquid out onto his hand, then offered the wineskin to Tishtry as he rubbed the wine into the feet of the statue as Drosos had done. Tishtry copied his motions, and as she watched the wine splash into the restless water, she hoped that the libation would gain them aid and favor from the elements.

"We're ready to get under way," Drosos told them as he gave his signal to the men handling the steering oars. "In good weather, we would make the crossing in nine or ten days, but with the wind the way it is, and the swell running heavy, it might be longer. If it goes badly, we can lay over at Athenae."

"Might it be necessary?" Tishtry asked, worry making her voice sharp.

The ship eased away from the dock, and the slaves on the mast pulled the square sail all the way down. Drosos signaled his approval with his arm and shook his head in answer to her question. "I've seen worse skies turn fine in an hour, and I've seen a squall come out of the sun. Pray that the gods favor us, and keep to your bunk if you're frightened."

"I'd rather stay with my team," Tishtry said, feeling her stomach lurch as the ship took the first frontal assault of the waves.

"That's your choice," Drosos said, then turned away toward the starboard steersman. "Hold on tight. We're going to have a rough ride."

Naius tugged Tishtry's sleeve. "Come on; leave them to their business and we'll tend to our own."

During the day the swell increased so that by sunset the merchantman was pitching heavily. Drosos had ordered the mainsail shortened some time before, and now he stood on the afterdeck, staring at the fading red of the western horizon. He rubbed his bearded face as he watched the movement of the sullen clouds. "We'll have a rough night," he predicted to the two steersmen. "You'll have to strap yourselves into your bunks."

The taller steersman, a swarthy, middle-aged man from Creta, agreed. "It will take both Lysander and Kortos to hold the ship on course tonight."

"And the cargo on deck will need tighter lashing to hold them in place," Drosos went on, thinking aloud. "Thank goodness we have no animals on the deck in cages. Just the horses are bad enough." He paused. "Do you recall the time that bear got loose during a storm?

I don't know which was worse, the wind or that animal."

"Best to warn the charioteers. They'll have to keep watch in the hold." The steersman pulled more tightly on his rudder. "Hey! Pari, keep a watch!"

The other steersman answered grimly, "I am. Tend to your side of the ship."

"No arguments," Drosos warned the men. "We have trouble enough without that. I wonder if it's worth putting out the lamps in this weather?"

"Better to have them. Who knows what other ships are out here on this night?" The Cretan leaned back to relieve the pressure on his arms, then set his grip more firmly.

Drosos muttered something to himself and went down into the hold, leaving his two steersmen to their task.

Tishtry was standing between two stalls, one arm wrapped around a supporting column, while she strove to quiet her team. "Don't be afraid, my heroes," she crooned to them, trying to reassure herself as much as the horses.

The horses, confined to slings in their stalls, were clearly distressed. Dozei had flecks of foam around his sling and Amath kept craning his neck and rolling his eyes. Immit let out a shrill, squealing whinny as the ship rocked and wallowed. Shirdas was making a useless attempt to kick his way out of his sling.

Naius, half drunk, sat slumped against the ramp to the deck. He was singing softly to himself, holding his wineskin as if it were a baby.

"I've come to warn you," Drosos said, raising his

112

voice to be heard over the horses and the moaning of the ship, "we're going to have to close this hatch. Otherwise we'll ship too much water. That means that you'll have to keep watch on the horses here—all of them, yours and the others—without help. I need all hands ready to fight the storm. Do you think you can take care of them?"

Tishtry, who had made a minor attempt to talk to the other horses in the hold, regarded the captain with dismay. "All of them?"

"I'm afraid so," Drosos answered, glancing down at Naius in disgust. "I can spare one man, perhaps. You might need him." He glowered at the man near his feet. "I don't think he'll be much use to you."

"Probably not," Tishtry agreed. She felt queasy, and the prospect of being enclosed in the hold while the ship weathered the storm was more terrifying than she could admit, even to herself. "The horses should have someone else to look after them."

"True enough," Drosos said. "I'll have one of the deck slaves come help you. Don't worry; he's good with horses. All my slaves are good with horses." He swung around and started back up the ramp, steadying himself with his hands as he went.

"Quite a ride, isn't it? Nothing like a chariot," Naius murmured, helping himself to more wine. "Think of how it will be tonight, all the water and the dark." He giggled.

There were shouted orders above them and the hatch cover was swung over the entrance to the ramp. Just before it closed, a small young man with a monkey face and tangled hair slipped through into the hold, reaching back to help batten the hatch into place.

Tishtry felt the dark close in around her and she had to resist the urge to bolt, to claw her way onto the deck, out of the dark confines of the hold. She swallowed hard, knowing that her team would sense her fear and become more distraught than they were already.

The monkey-faced deck slave made his way toward Tishtry. "The captain sent me to help out, charioteer," he said with a strong Baetican accent. "We'll take care of the horses, you and I."

Tishtry nodded, then realized he would not see the movement. "Of course," she forced herself to say, as if she were as used to being on a ship as he was. "The pregnant mare, the yellow one, not the other, is very restless. She's in the fourth stall from the end."

"I'll go to her," the Baetican said, making his way down the narrow corridor between the stalls. "Your comrade has been foolish."

"Worse than that," Tishtry said. She was still shocked at how Naius had behaved since they had boarded the ship, but her reaction, if any, would have to wait until the storm was over.

All through the night the ship was battered by waves. Tishtry could hear water break over the prow and rush down the decks. In spite of the hatch covers, trickles spattered down on her. She tried not to notice them, and as she grew more exhausted, she did not. At the suggestion of the Baetican, she began to move from one stall to another, patting the horses, checking their slings, and talking to them. At first she disliked the duty, then she took comfort in it, because it kept her mind from the storm and made it impossible for her to fall asleep from utter fatigue.

When the night was almost over, one of the other horses, a big Galatian stallion with a spotted coat and a bad temper, broke one side of his sling in his struggles. Immediately he began to scramble on the floor, trying for better purchase on the straw-littered boards; he lashed out with teeth and hooves at anything that touched him. The other horses, already near panic, began to struggle even more desperately, straining at the slings that held them.

"Get him! Get him!" the Baetican slave shouted to Tishtry. "You're nearer."

"I can't! He's too wild!"

"Take a stick and hit him" came the order. "Hard! The others will break free if this keeps up much longer."

The Galatian stallion bucked and twisted, trying to get out of the one remaining support of his sling. His hooves thundered against the side of his stall, splintering the wood and making the horse beside him paw the air with his hooves.

"Stop him, stop him, *stop him!*" the Baetican slave yelled, barely audible over the sound of the storm and the horses.

At last Tishtry found a length of wood and seized it in her free hand. She could not reach the stallion from where she was, and she was afraid to get too much closer, for there was danger from the maddened horse. There was almost no light in the hold, just the faint, wavering illumination of two oil lamps that swung as the ship rose and fell. It was very chancy. She could feel her pulse drum in her ears, rapid and hard, like a fist pounding at her skull. She knew she was terrified. Vainly she tried to recall her father's voice, exhorting her to go on, to steady her nerves and take the risk.

"Hang on!" the Baetican slave bellowed at her as the ship swooped down the side of a wave. Beams groaned and the planks shuddered under the impact.

Tishtry latched her arm around another upright post, swinging as she was nearly thrown off her feet. The horse in the stall beside her flailed in his sling.

"Now. It's easier now!" the young man urged.

Tishtry pulled herself one stall closer to the struggling Galatian stallion. She almost lost her grip on the wood she carried as the ship plunged through another wave. With all her strength she braced herself, then swung with the club.

Her first blow went wild and she wanted to scream with vexation. That, she told herself inwardly, would only make matters worse. The second time she brought the wood up, she drove it toward the head of the stallion, and felt her arm shudder as the club struck home.

The stallion shrieked, kicked viciously, then stumbled and fell heavily onto his side.

Tishtry stood, aghast at her act.

"Good!" the Baetican shouted to her. "Now we have some chance of saving the others."

Wearily Tishtry righted herself and started toward the next stall, where one of the mares had succeeded in tangling her rear leg in her sling. The habit of years kept her to her work as she went from horse to horse.

Morning was more than half gone by the time the worst of the storm let up. The winds were still high, but no longer blowing in unpredictable gusts; now they were steady, filling the sails and shoving the merchantman farther to the south than it would usually go.

"You did very well," the Baetican slave told Tishtry as they leaned against the bulkhead together. Most of the horses were calmer, a few of them even willing to eat from nosebags.

"That stallion . . ." Tishtry said, hardly able to look at where the big spotted horse had fallen.

"The others would have broken free if you had not done it," the young man reminded her. "The horses would have injured themselves or been killed, and they could have damaged the ship. One horse is not a great price to pay for the lives of all the others." He patted her shoulder, this rough gesture showing his respect. "There's many sailors who could not have done as well as you did."

Tishtry sighed. "Still, I wish I had not had to do it. He was a beautiful animal, and it's such a waste." Her shoulders ached as if she had been dragged by her team around the arena, and now that she was more accustomed to the motion of the ship, she was more hungry than she could ever remember being. The only need greater than her need for food was her desire for sleep. "How much longer do we have to wait here?"

"Until the captain opens the hatch and tells us that we can leave." He looked contemptuously at Naius, who lay snoring in the corner. "That one is worse than useless."

117

Tishtry only nodded. "The mare, the one who caught her leg in the sling?—she's got a sprain, I think. I'll put a poultice on it in a little while, so that it won't stiffen up on her."

"You can do that after you've rested," the Baetican slave said.

"I'd better do that before. I feel as if I'll sleep for a week." She moved away from the bulkhead. "There are rags in my chest, if you'll bring some to me. And there's a leather pouch, dyed green, with herbs in it. I'll use them to make a poultice if the cook can spare some olive oil."

"I'll ask as soon as we're let out." He scrambled to his feet. His tunica was torn and its belt had come untied sometime in the night. There were smudges on his face and a long cut on his forearm where he had scraped himself in an effort to get away from a nasty kick. Looking at him, Tishtry wondered if she was as bedraggled as he was.

Naius coughed and rolled over, spilling the rest of the contents of his wineskin over the damp planking.

"Your master should flog him," the Baetican said.

"My master is not very decisive," Tishtry said, smiling faintly. "I don't think he punishes his slaves very often."

"And see what such laxness brings," the young man observed. "A slave who is a sot."

"Naius was that long before my master owned him," Tishtry pointed out. "He has been this way for many years, or so I heard the others say when I was still . . . home."

There was a subtle shift in the movement of the ship

through the water. The Baetican slave cocked his head to the side. "We're turning. We're moving more to the north. The storm must have driven us farther south than the usual course."

"What does that mean?" Tishtry asked. She looked up at the closed hatch as if the force of her eyes would move it.

"Who knows? It may bring us to shore more quickly, if Drosos wishes to stop at Athenae. If he does not, then we might add a day to the voyage. The wind has come around to our back, which gives us speed, but it can be very dangerous. Drosos has great skill, but the sea is a dangerous master." He ran his hands through his hair. "Am I a complete disgrace?"

"Am I?" Tishtry asked.

The Baetican laughed. "No doubt we're *both* a disgrace." Then he shrugged. "What is your name?"

"Tishtry," she told him.

"I'm Holik."

For some reason, this struck both of them as very amusing; first they chuckled, then laughed, then all but fell to the floor with guffaws that bordered on tears. As Tishtry clutched her sides, some part of her realized that her reaction was more the product of terror and fatigue than of anything funny, but she made no effort to stop herself until the laughter ended of its own volition. Gradually the manic humor left them both, and they sat, more tired than ever, and stared dazedly at each other.

"Holik," Tishtry said, and this time the name was only a name. No strange mirth rose to her lips.

"Tishtry," he said, nodding to her. "You would have

been a good sailor, girl, if you were male and not a charioteer."

Her smile was genuine. "Thank you."

There was a sound above them of the upper battens being drawn back. Holik scrambled to his feet and helped lift the heavy cover from the hatch.

Drosos looked down on them, worry on his tanned and creased countenance. "Is all well in here?"

"The Galatian stallion got loose," Holik said at once. "Tishtry was able to strike him with a club."

"I'm afraid he's badly hurt. Or dead," she admitted.

"Just one?" Drosos said, his shaggy brows going up in disbelief. "You must be very lucky or you worked harder than anyone on this ship." He sighed. "We lost two slaves overboard in the night. They were reefing the sails when we hit a bad swell. Even if we could have gone back, in such heavy seas, there would have been no way to find them."

Holik nodded. "Two men, one horse."

Drosos shrugged philosophically. "I've had worse luck in better weather. Come. You will want to have food and rest."

Tishtry almost succumbed to this temptation, but she controlled the yawn that lay in her throat. "I want to make a poultice first. One of the mares has a bad sprain." She reached up to take Drosos' hand and climbed out of the hold onto the sunny, wind-scoured deck. "I'll rest after that."

"If that's what you want," Drosos said, already turning his attention to the ripped sail that flapped overhead. "Holik will help you."

120

As she started after the Baetican slave, Tishtry doubted she could keep her eyes open long enough to find her bunk, let alone prepare the poultice. She stumbled once, and then steeled herself to her work. Soon, she promised herself as she got out the green leather pouch. Soon you will sleep. Soon. Soon.

CHAPTER

XI

After five days, they rounded the end of Achaea and turned northwest, going up the Mare Adriaticum. The weather, after such a ferocious beginning, steadied and held fine, with a good breeze and untroubled waters.

To Tishtry's surprise, she began to enjoy the voyage, and often spent several hours on deck, watching the distant land slide by.

"That's Macedonia," Holik told her as he pointed out the mountains that seemed to rise out of the edge of the sea. "And beyond is Illyricum. We stop first at Apollonia, in Macedonia. It will be two days at the most from Apollonia to Salonae."

"If there isn't another storm," she cautioned.

"True." He cuffed her shoulder. "You'd take it in stride, though."

Tishtry shrugged. She was grateful to the young Baetican, for he had appointed himself her friend and her helper. The aid was as welcome as it was unexpected, but she accepted it without question, since she knew she would have no assistance from Naius. "Let us hope it will not be necessary."

Holik grinned. "Fair skies and calm seas all the way."

"Good." Tishtry realized with a pang that she would miss him when she reached Salonae.

"Your horses are getting restive," Holik commented when a whinny was heard from the open hatch.

"It's the inactivity. Even with reduced food, they do not like being kept in those slings. They're used to running every day, and working on the lunge. To be confined for so long is strange to them." She turned her face up to the sky. "It would be a good day to race, today."

Holik gave her a friendly, inquiring glance. "Why?"

"It's warm but not hot, the sun is bright but there is little glare, and there is enough wind to give freshness but not enough to raise dust." She leaned on the barrier of heavy, knotted ropes that stretched along the side of the ship above the wooden railing. "What is the purpose of these?"

"They let the seas wash over us but catch any cargo that might come loose," Holik explained. "There are drains at six places on the deck, but these assure us that we will not ship too much water in heavy seas. And you know for yourself how important that can be."

"Yes," she said with a touch of grimness in her voice. "I know."

"Neptune and the winds were kind to us. They did not blow away the sails, or the masts. Drosos is a good captain, and he is sensible enough to take the most

123

prudent course; not like some who would try to battle the storm with a full hold. There are not many merchantmen that would have come through the storm as well as we have done." He beamed with pride, his monkey face showing weathered creases already. Tishtry, watching him, thought that he would be as brown and wrinkled as a walnut before he was thirty. "You will have something to boast of when you arrive in Salonae."

Tishtry shrugged. "I don't boast. It's a bad business in the arena. It makes the others test you and trap you. Men have died on the sands for a boast."

"But how many of them have been in a storm like the one you have come through?" He looked off toward the shore. "We'll be turning soon. Apollonia is not far ahead now. By nightfall we'll be at the dock."

"And I can walk on something that doesn't move all the time," Tishtry said with relief.

"You drive a quadriga," Holik pointed out.

"Hardly the same thing. The ground under the wheels is stable enough." She smiled. "And then Salonae. I wonder if Naius will be sober enough to find his way to the amphitheater by then?"

"He won't be if he goes on as he has been going," Holik cautioned her. "Don't depend on him for much, Tishtry. Men of his sort are poor risks."

"Yes; I know." She looked at the Baetican slave. "I'd prefer having you about than Naius."

"Slaves cannot choose such things," Holik said, a bitterness at the back of his eyes. "Still, in time I will have enough to buy my freedom, and then I will do as I wish."

"What *do* you intend to do, when you are free?" Tishtry asked him.

"I would like to have a little shop where I could sell equipment and material to merchants: ropes, sails, oil lamps, netting, all the fittings for a good ship like this one." His expression warmed as he spoke.

"It costs money to start a shop," Tishtry remarked.

"It does. But Drosos has agreed to be my partner when I am free. He will provide the money to start, and I will pay him thirty percent of my profits until the loan is paid off, and twenty-five percent thereafter." Now he grinned. "It isn't an uncommon arrangement."

Tishtry had heard of many similar agreements. "I hope it goes well for you, Holik."

"And I hope it goes well for you, Tishtry." He cuffed her on the shoulder once more. "I have to go aloft. And it's time you watered your horses again."

"Yes," she said, reluctant to leave the deck and Holik's company. "Perhaps we'll talk later."

"All right," he said, reaching for one of the thick hempen lines that ran to the top of the mast.

She watched him climb, then went down into the hold to tend to her team and the other horses confined there.

The layover in Apollonia was brief, and Drosos was under way again before the sun had set. He had left off eight of the horses he carried, and now the ship was light in the water, skimming along briskly. The crew were in good spirits and they called jokes to one another while they went about their tasks. The two steersmen sang as they held on course, and even Drosos made a witty remark or two while he issued his orders.

Tishtry sat near the afterdeck, staring up at the sails and the stars beyond. The movement of the vessel was comfortable to her now, and she felt happily relaxed. It would be over before night fell again, she told herself sternly, and she would have to get her horses and herself back into form for racing and doing tricks. The storm had frightened her, and she still winced when she thought of clubbing the maddened stallion, but for the most part, her voyage had been pleasant and, except for Naius, enjoyable. At the thought of that ruin of a man, she tightened her jaw. While she was in Salonae, he would be in charge of her, and she did not like the idea. Still, her master had sent him and given him authority, and she could not defy those orders without serious consequences. She leaned back on her elbows. She would have to find a way to guard herself against him, for he had threatened to hurt her more than once. Nothing had happened so far because Drosos and his crew had prevented it. That protection would be gone shortly and she would have to find other means to deal with him.

"Merchantman ahead!" called one of the steersman.

Tishtry got to her feet and went to the side of the boat, peering across the water to another dark shape, like a shadow in the afterglow of sunset. It was headed west.

"Bound from Dyrrhachium to Ancona by the look of her," Drosos shouted to his crew. "Probably carrying olive oil and linen. She's small and light."

The other steersman pointed away in the dusk toward the shore where a light gleamed. "The Dyrrhachium lighthouse."

"We're doing well," Drosos announced with great goodwill.

The steersmen went back to singing their playful, rollicking songs. Listening to them, Tishtry fell asleep on deck, where Drosos found her near the middle of the night.

He chuckled. "You'd do well at sea, girl," he said softly, and did not disturb her, letting the rising sun wake her.

Salonae was large and the dock so busy that it took a little time for Drosos to find a berth where he could offload his cargo. Tishtry was alarmed by the constant bustle on the dock and the quay; she confided her feelings to Holik.

"Don't worry—the crew will watch your belongings while you tend to your team. But it is wise to be careful of thieves, for the harbor has more of them than rats, I think."

Tishtry took little comfort from this warning, and her apprehension increased when Naius ambled down the gangplank to where her quadriga waited.

"There's a tavern close by. You'll find me there," he told her as he strolled away.

"What tavern?" she called after him.

"It has a sign showing a spotted dog. It's two streets farther on. Ask anyone; they'll tell you how to find it." Then he was gone in the jostle of the crowd and Tishtry felt a helplessness she had never known before.

"Here," Holik said as he came to her side. "You go get your horses and I'll see that no one takes your chest or your quadriga."

"Thanks," she said, bolting back for the ship. "I'll bring them out as quickly as I can."

Belowdecks, most of the crew were busy getting the horses out of their slings and starting them up the ramp. Most of the horses were in bad tempers from their long stay in the hold, and a few of them kicked and bucked as they were released.

Tishtry found Drosos attempting to bridle Immit, and she took over for him. "She's more used to me," she explained.

"I'll get the bay, if that's agreeable," the captain said with a twinkle in his eyes. "They're good-looking animals, this team of yours."

It was pleasant to hear someone speak well of them without criticizing their lack of uniform coloring, and Tishtry blushed. "I have always thought so."

"Is Holik coming to help?" Drosos inquired as he released the sling holding the bay.

"He's guarding my chest and quadriga on the dock." She paused, working the cheek strap on Immit's bridle. "Naius has gone to find wine."

"That should not surprise you," Drosos said gently.

"It doesn't, but it troubles me. My master has said that I am to obey Naius, but how can I do that when the man is . . . what he is?"

Drosos nodded as he bridled Amath. "A pity, but surely your master had a good reason to send the man."

"He used to race everywhere, but that was some time ago," Tishtry said, shaking her head as she stood back to lead Immit out of the stall.

"Before he took to wine, I've no doubt," Drosos said.

"Here. You may have this one, too." He handed Amath's reins to Tishtry. "Let the mare go first; she's more restless."

Tishtry accepted this advice willingly, backing up the ramp as she led her horses out onto the deck and to the gangplank. Immit and Amath minced across it, their hooves loud on the wood. The crowd on the pier upset them, and their ears swiveled uneasily.

"Give them to me," Holik said, reaching for the reins.

"Be sure they don't get too much of a lead on you," Tishtry warned as she handed the horses over to him. "I'm going back for Shirdas and Dozei. I won't be long."

"I've ordered a cart to carry your quadriga. Four-horse rigs aren't allowed within the city walls at this time of day. You'll have to walk the horses to the amphitheater and have the quadriga carried," Holik called to her as she hurried back across the gangplank.

"Very well!" she shouted as she went back into the hold.

"Here they are." Drosos was waiting for her, the two remaining horses out of their slings and bridled. "The rest of the grain you brought on board for them is in that barrel, and I'll have Kortos bring it out to you." He looked at her with concern and respect. "You're a worthy girl. I hope the gods show you favor."

"And you, Captain," she answered, holding the reins as her horses pulled at the leather. "Come to see me in the arena, if you have the chance."

"I would like that. Perhaps on the return voyage. I have an order to pick up a dozen lions in Tyrus. Twenty days out, twenty days back, you should still be performing then, shouldn't you?" He chucked her under the chin with his hard, square hand. "I will look forward to watching you."

Tishtry could not quite smile, but she nodded. "I will do well for you, if you come to watch me." She gave him her thumb up, and tugged her horses toward the ramp before she felt too foolish.

"They're being pretty temperamental," Holik said as he cocked his head toward Amath and Immit. "It's been difficult to hold them."

"You've done well," Tishtry said, having her own task with Shirdas and Dozei. "I'll take them in a moment."

"You'll never get them to the arena on your own." He paused. "Drosos will permit me to help you, if you would like me to ask."

Tishtry sighed. "It ought to be Naius, but . . . If Drosos is willing, I would be grateful for your help. I'll have to look for Naius later, once I've found where I am to stable my team." She looked about in exasperation, not knowing where the amphitheater was, or how to get there.

Holik guessed her thoughts. "The carter will lead us. Carters always know the best ways through the streets. On a day like this, his help will be welcome."

"More than Naius', probably," she said in an irritated tone. As Dozei tried to toss his head, Tishtry reached up and patted him, smoothing the hair on his neck and tugging his mane affectionately. She could feel his pent-up energy through the rein. The arch of his neck alerted her to his excitement after so many inactive days. "Steady, boy. In a little while you'll be in a stall, and this evening

I'll work you on the lunge until your sides ache."

Dozei lowered his head and nudged her arm with his nose.

Holik pointed through the crowd. "I see the carter coming. I warn you, he speaks no Armenian or Greek, just Latin."

"I suppose I'll have to learn more Latin," Tishtry said wearily. She had spoken Armenian and Greek most of her life but had never been comfortable with the Roman language. "Will you give him the order for me? I don't want to make a mess of it."

"He already knows where you're going," Holik said, waving with the ends of the reins to attract the man's attention. "Not that there would be any doubt, with four horses and a quadriga. Where else could you be going?" He glanced back toward the ship. "Captain!" he shouted as Drosos emerged from the hold. "I'm going to help Tishtry get her horses and gear to the amphitheater!"

"Fine!" Drosos responded at once. "Make sure she's expected! Don't leave her until she's in the hands of the Master of the Bestiarii!"

"I will," Holik promised, then addressed the carter in Latin as awkward as Tishtry's. "We must go to . . . to—"

"To the amphitheater," the carter agreed, looking over the quadriga and chest that waited beside Tishtry and Holik. "Is there anything more?"

"A barrel of grain," Tishtry said at once. "For the horses."

The carter nodded. "I'll wait while you get it." He looked over the horses with a suspicious expression.

131

"What do you do? You don't race them, do you?"

"I do tricks," Tishtry corrected him sharply.

"With a team like that, I'd suppose so," the carter said, chortling. "They're a bit of a trick themselves, aren't they?" He saw Kortos come with the barrel. "Is that all of it?"

"That's all," Tishtry said.

"Then I'll bring my cart. Your horses won't mind my mule, will they?" He gave her very little chance to answer. "I won't have those brutes of yours kicking my mule and that's that."

"They won't kick your mule," Tishtry assured him, adding to Holik in Greek, "We'll let him lead us. You go first and I'll come after."

"Good," the carter interrupted in dreadful Greek. "And that way, no harm will come to my mule."

"If that's what you want," Holik said to Tishtry, ignoring the carter.

Tishtry said a few more soothing words to her horses, hoping that they would indeed mind their manners when the carter brought his mule. After all that time at sea, she was afraid that they might be too rambunctious to behave as well as they usually did. "Don't let them have their heads. They're going to try to shake loose, but don't let them," she instructed Holik.

"I'll try," he said, looking uneasily at the reins. "They're strong, aren't they?"

"The line on a taut sail is worse," she said, trying to find the carter among all the other people. "Where is he?"

"Give him a little time. He can't clear a path by

galloping, Tishtry.'' He was silent, but there was plainly something on his mind.

''What is it?'' she asked when he had been fretting over it.

''I . . . I'll miss you. I liked sailing with you. That's all.'' Under his dark tan, his face was rosy.

Tishtry had to blink back sudden tears. She had not wanted to think of saying good-bye to Holik, and now he had reminded her that they would part before the day was over and might never see each other again. ''I'm not gone yet,'' she said gruffly to cover the loneliness she felt. ''But you were good to me. I am grateful for that.''

Holik stared down at his feet. ''I won't forget you, Tishtry, not ever. And when you're famous, I'll tell everyone that we sailed together when you were on your way to Salonae. They won't believe me, but that won't stop me telling them.''

Tishtry coughed, but the tightness in her throat did not go away. ''I might overturn my chariot and be sent back to Barantosz in disgrace. You never know.''

''You'll be famous. I can tell. They'll all cheer you, every one, and you'll be honored by the Emperor himself.'' His voice dropped to a mumble.

At this Tishtry laughed while she felt color suffuse her face. ''There are times I dream of it,'' she confessed. ''But when I am awake, I can't imagine Nero bothering over someone like me. He has a chance to see the best that the entire Roman Empire can offer.''

''Well, you are fine,'' Holik said doggedly.

''You've never seen me in the arena. You've never

133

seen me on a horse," she reminded him, though her pleasure was greater than her pride at the touching faith he showed in her.

"It doesn't matter. I've seen you in a storm at sea, and that tells me all I need to know." His chin was thrust out as if he were angry with her, not paying her a compliment.

"There's the carter," she said, relieved that they would not have to say anything more to each other that would make them both uncomfortable.

"Here," the carter said as he brought his mule close to them. "One of you hold the horses and the other help me load up. You'd better hold the horses, girl; they tell me they're yours."

Tishtry did as he said, glad that she was about to get back to the work she knew best. As soon as the cart was loaded, Holik came and took Dozei and Amath from her without saying a word. Tishtry was both comforted and distressed by this. It was best that they say little, she reminded herself. They had to reconcile themselves to parting, and it was easier if they did not reveal too much to each other. This sensible attitude could not keep her from being downcast as she followed the carter and Holik through the crowded, narrow streets of Salonae.

CHAPTER

XII

Chimbue Barantosz arrived in Salonae six weeks after Tishtry, flustered by the voyage and distressed by the size of the city. "They say you need more training," he complained to Tishtry after she had finished performing for the day. "Naius says it, and two of the other bestiarii say it. They tell me you're too good not to have the training." He rubbed his squat hands together and shook his head so that his jowls wobbled like dewlaps.

"I do," Tishtry said. She had realized it as soon as she had seen what the other trick riders could do. She wiped her forehead with the back of her wrist, wishing she had been permitted to bathe before seeing her master.

"But you're so much better than you were," he said, clearly not understanding the problem.

"And if I am to go further, I must be better still. The charioteers here have told me that they like what I do, but they do not think I am ready to advance. Find me a teacher, and I will learn everything I can." She put her hands on her hips. "And I do need two more horses."

"I can't afford them," Barantosz protested. "By the demons of the air, you don't know what you have cost me already."

"Give me the reckoning, and I will know," Tishtry said, since she had a little knowledge of counting.

"It is not so simple," Barantosz countered evasively. He lay back on his couch, fanning his face. "The Legions have been slow to purchase horses. They want more mules, and here I am with twenty-three mares in foal. You could not have chosen a worse time to need anything from me."

Tishtry was wise enough to say nothing in answer to this blustering. She changed the subject deliberately. "I have been taking time to improve my Latin. Most of the arena slaves use Greek, but if I am to do more, the Latin will help."

"Yes, yes," he said absently. "That is wise of you."

"But it will be of more use to me if I have the opportunity to advance," she pointed out, bringing her master back to the matter at hand.

He made pudgy little fists of his hands. "You pester me and pester me, and I can't think when you do that."

"I didn't mean to pester you," Tishtry said quickly. "It is only that I am anxious to justify your faith in me."

"Of course, yes." He sat up again, his face turning plum color. "I do not know what I can do, girl. You will have to wait, that's all. Until I make more money from the horses, you will simply have to wait."

Tishtry's heart turned cold, for she knew that Barantosz could procrastinate for years, and in that time she would lose the advantage her youth gave her. "Master, I beg you to reconsider. If you wish me to bring you more money, you must give me the opportunity to do more. As it stands, I am caught here, and there is nothing I can do that will . . ."

Barantosz waved her to silence. "You are not to talk to me this way. I own you, girl."

"You could sell me," she said before she could stop herself. As soon as the words were out, she caught her lower lip in her teeth.

"Stop talking nonsense!" Barantosz ordered her. "Your father will not want to hear that you have lost all sense of conduct."

"My father . . ." Tishtry wanted to have news of Soduz, but had dared not ask. How she longed to know how her family were doing, who was well, who had been ill!

"He's in good fettle now that his ankle is better," Barantosz said, and volunteered no more information. "Go away, Tishtry. I am tired from my journey. I will speak to you later."

Tishtry withdrew, worried, and feeling very alone as she wandered back toward the stables where her team was kept.

"So you saw the master, did you?" Naius asked maliciously. "You won't get him to invest more in you, you know that." He held up his half-finished skin of wine. "Want some?"

"No. I have to exercise my team still." They had been cooled by the stable hands, but Tishtry had taken to working them on the lunge after they had performed.

She thought it made them less nervous, but was wise enough to know that it might be only her nerves that were soothed by the exercise.

"Too bad that Roman didn't convince the master to sell you. He might have been willing to get you a coach. Barantosz is likely to send you home in a year and breed you." He drank from the wineskin. "Don't take it too badly. Barantosz would deny anyone." With a rude gesture, he was gone.

Tishtry walked to the door of Dozei's stall and looked in at the sorrel. "You were spooked today," she said to her horse. "That isn't like you."

Dozei turned his head and looked at Tishtry, his huge brown eyes regarding her steadily. Then he snorted and waggled his head before stretching down to nibble at the straw.

"Don't blame the horses," Naius said behind her. "They can't help it when the crowd is noisy. You're the one who has to keep them steady. They're just animals, and it's up to you to guide them."

This was more than Tishtry could stand. "Be quiet!" she grated.

"Oh-ho!" Naius teased. "Getting miffed, are you? Annoyed because the master wouldn't be convinced to do what you want?"

"Stop it!" Her voice was louder and more ragged. "Right now."

"Now, now, don't get touchy," he chided her. "That's not the way to get me to help you, is it?"

"I don't want you to help me, not after what you've done." She could feel tears hot in her eyes and she wanted to run away from him, to be alone in the sudden rush of misery that threatened to overcome her. She had to convince Barantosz to get her a coach, she *had* to. Otherwise she might never be able to earn enough to buy her family's freedom. It was unthinkable that she would let them down after all they had done for her. She had to admit that she was galled to be held back as much as she was infuriated by the thought of failure.

"My, my, turning temperamental, aren't you?"

"You want to make it worse," she accused him, and knew from his grin that she was right.

"You should learn to be patient, girl, and to be more flexible, more accommodating. Otherwise you will gain enemies. Slaves cannot afford to have enemies." He sucked at the mouth of the wineskin, watching her as a little of the red liquid dribbled down his chin.

"Leave me alone, Naius." She felt fatigue now, more consuming than her anger had been. "I have to have some time to myself."

"Surely," he said, giving her a mocking inclination of his head. "And when you're ready to be sensible, you come talk to me again, all right? Between us we should be able to arrange something."

She had already turned away from him, going toward the tack room at the far end of the stable, where she could occupy herself with waxing her bridles instead of dwelling on her growing sense of disappointment.

For a week, Barantosz refused to speak to Tishtry again, finding a variety of excuses to avoid her. She knew from the few tidbits of gossip Naius offered that Barantosz had been asking many questions about her, but to what end, Naius refused to say. When he bothered to mention anything, it was with the snide reminder that she would have to abide by their master's decision, whatever it was.

Tishtry tried to put her concern about this new development out of her mind by spending more time working with her team, working with them vigorously and drilling them while she practiced handstands and somersaults on their backs, driving herself into a fatigue so deep that she could not spend her nights in sleepless pondering. On the eighth day of this routine, she discovered a stranger sitting on the fence of the practice ring watching her.

"You handle them very well," he said when Tishtry took a break.

"Thank you," she said, paying little attention to him. There were many strangers in Salonae, and those who came to the amphitheater often spent an idle hour observing bestiarii and charioteers in training, since they were forbidden to watch the fighters—gladiators, retiarii, secutores, essedarii, and captured soldiers from every client nation of the Empire. She had learned early to pay no heed to such spectators.

"I like the team. They're innovative." He motioned to Immit. "They say pale horses aren't lucky."

"I haven't found it so," Tishtry answered, noting the man's collar and wondering whose slave he was.

He watched as she prepared to work Dozei on the lunge. "I'm an aurigatore, called Himic. I raced before I broke my leg."

She whistled Dozei out to the end of the lunge and

began to take him through his paces, watching him critically.

"I saw your quadriga in the arena yesterday. A bit old-fashioned, isn't it?"

Although Tishtry agreed with him, she knew better than to admit it. "It is what my master provides me."

"Ah." He was content to sit still for a time. "You have marvelous hands."

"I have to have. I couldn't do what I do without them," she responded, forcing Dozei to lengthen his trot without breaking into a canter.

"Your inner horse, the chestnut; he's in need of more oil on his hooves. They look too dry, and that might cause them to split." He offered this in the most helpful voice. "You have to pardon me for speaking out, but since I became an aurigatore, I notice things like hooves and the state of your tack and quadriga."

"Not surprising," Tishtry said, trying not to be brusque with the man, for she felt very much in need of a friend, and thought perhaps this older slave would sympathize with her but not shame her with pity.

"Do you think your horses could learn to do more than their usual paces?" He had not spoken for a little while, and his question, so unexpected, startled Tishtry.

"I don't know. I never thought about it. They will rear together if I force them, but that's about it." She went to unfasten the lunge and transfer it to Amath.

"I see." He remained quiet while she worked Amath, contenting himself with studying the way she handled the dark bay. He made only one suggestion, which again interested Tishtry. "You might try a different set of sig-

141

nals. The whistle you give for slowing down is very like what some of the audience do when they want to urge a team on in a race. You don't race in competition, but it might confuse your animals."

Tishtry turned toward Himic again. "I'll bear that in mind," she said, warming to the stranger. "But it's not easy to change them once they've learned something," she could not resist pointing out.

"They can be trained, with patience." He came down off the high rail into the ring. "Let me look at that chestnut's feet, will you?"

Her first reaction was to refuse, but she had been hungry for some trace of companionship; this older man was the first who seemed genuine in his interest and his attitude. She thought it over. "All right. But be careful going near him, he's a little head shy."

"I noticed that," Himic said with a smile. "But you were good to tell me. There's many another who would have let me tangle with him." He went toward Shirdas at a steady pace, talking quietly as he went.

Tishtry nodded as she watched him. There was no doubt that the man knew what he was doing around horses, unlike some who claimed to be expert and were not. She waited while he bent over the lifted hooves, trying them one at a time. "What do you think?" she asked when Himic was through.

"Several breeds have trouble running on sand. It's too dry, and it's hard on their hooves. You've done a good job of keeping them filed—you are the one who does that, aren't you?—but they need oil on them as well." He brushed off his hands against his tunica and the loose leggings he wore under them. "I have a preparation of wool fat and ground seaweed that I will give you for him."

Tishtry blinked. "Why would you do that for me?"

Himic did not answer at once. "My master has offered to buy you from your master. He has said that I am to be your aurigatore. If anything were to happen to your team between now and then, he would be displeased with me, and I don't want that to happen."

"Your master is buying me? Who is your master?" Tishtry was completely baffled now, as if she had somehow forgotten something very important. "I know nothing of this."

"Well, the arrangements haven't been concluded yet, but my master is confident that Barantosz will sell you." He folded his arms and looked down at her. "And my master is willing to see that you have the extra horses you need and a proper chariot for your tricks, not the quadriga you currently use."

"I see," Tishtry said, though she did not see at all.

"It is a good thing for you that this man is a generous fool," Barantosz scolded Tishtry as he watched her remove his collar. "I would not accept an offer for you under ordinary circumstances, but the way my luck has been, and the expenses I have had, I cannot afford to keep you any longer, not without seeing more of a profit from you than I have done. This man seems to believe that you will earn him much money, which I have already warned him may not be the case. Nevertheless, he is persistent, and he has money enough to throw away on an arena slave like you. So be it." He slapped his thigh in exasperation. "I have agreed to send Atadillius his fee for your sale, since it was he who brought you to this new master's attention. That will be an obligation you will have, to justify the price Calpurnius has paid for you.''

"Calpurnius?'' Tishtry repeated, recalling the Roman who had talked to her in Troas.

"Gnaeus Calpurnius, a Roman tribune; he has seen you in the arena before and he believes he can make something of you.'' Barantosz lifted his hands to show that he was innocent of such foolishness. "You are to continue here for a time, and then he will make other arrangements for you. If you do not live up to his expectations, he may sell you again, or breed you, hoping your children will be worth the money he has spent.'' He reached for the pitcher of wine that stood on the table in the arbor where they sat. "You have much to be thankful for, Tishtry, and I think you should let your new master know of it as soon as possible.'' He glared at her.

"What of my family? Will I still be able to purchase their freedom?'' She felt stiff as she asked the question, and her tongue seemed too large for her mouth. "I gave my word that I—''

"Yes; yes. I remember all about that, and I have turned enough profit on your sale not to interfere with your plans.'' He paused. "And it is Roman law that you are entitled to purchase your freedom and the freedom of your family, and funds for that purpose cannot be taken or taxed or confiscated by anyone. Calpurnius reminded me of this, though I am well aware of it.'' His features turned sulky. "The price for your family was fixed and I cannot change it. You may be sure that

144

you will have to pay the amount we agreed upon, and no more. If one of your father's two wives has another child, well, that will be for him to settle with me, but I swear that I will not sell him or any of his family for five more years. I will accept no offer from anyone else, and I will say so. That is part of the contract of your sale, and Calpurnius will enter it in his contract, if he should sell you." He drank most of his wine at one gulp. "There. Are you satisfied?"

Tishtry did not know what to say in answer. She looked at the new collar that was waiting for her, and saw her new master's name inscribed on it. "I am grateful, Master."

"Call Calpurnius that now. And by all the gods of the sky, do not do anything that will bring him dishonor or shame. You are to be willing and cooperative with him, and to . . ." He stared past her toward the wall of the compound that stood beside the amphitheater. "He can help me sell horses, this Calpurnius. If he is well disposed toward me, it will do much to improve my fortunes. Remember that, and remember that I still own your family."

"I will not forget," she vowed, unsure of the threat in Barantosz's words.

"You are to be sent tonight to the villa of Salvius Virginius Marco, where you will be told what your master expects of you. Your team will stay where it is, since it is Calpurnius' intention to have you perform here for a little longer." He indicated the new collar. "Put that on, or must I have one of my slaves do it for you?"

Obediently, she picked up the silver collar and placed

145

it around her neck, saying as she did, "I will conduct myself honorably, Barantosz. You have no need to fear that I won't."

Barantosz sighed. "You had better. I have too much to gain from your new owner to tolerate any difficulty from you." He turned away from her. "Now hurry; Calpurnius will want to talk with you."

"As you wish," Tishtry said, feeling a bit dizzy as she left the arbor. So she was now a slave of the Roman tribune Gnaeus Calpurnius. What would that mean to her?

Barantosz's voice came after her as she walked away. "And for the gods of the air, improve your Latin!"

CHAPTER

XIII

"That's still not good enough!" Himic shouted as Tishtry pulled her horses through a narrow gate set up in the practice ring. "You're letting Shirdas tug the others, and that's not right!"

Tishtry jumped back into the lightweight chariot and drew the team to a halt. "It's better than it's ever been before," she protested stubbornly.

Himic responded mildly, "I'm not arguing that; but it's still not good enough. You can do better, and I expect that you will."

"Is that an order?" she demanded.

"Our master can order you—I can only instruct." He approached her. "In eight weeks you have done very well, girl, but you have better in you, and Calpurnius has said that he will want you to be at your best form when you enter the arena again."

"Whenever that is," Tishtry said glumly. When Calpurnius had withdrawn her from performance, she expected her recess to be brief, but it had stretched now to almost two months and there was no end in sight. She had begun to resent the time she practiced, since it seemed to serve no purpose.

"I will tell him when I believe you are prepared enough," Himic said, as he had said many times before. "You have done well, remember that."

She touched her new chariot. "This is better than the old one; I'll grant that, and it's lighter. That's part of the problem," she admitted. "I haven't got used to how light it is, and that throws my timing off."

"Naturally," Himic said, limping beside her as she took her horses at a walk around the ring. "But you must master the chariot before you get the new horses you wish. That is our master's decision, and we must abide by it." He signaled her to go on. "Make them trot together. Their paces are good, but they must drill like soldiers if you are to seem anything more than a clever barbarian to the Romans."

She sighed, but did her best to make her team move in unison. She noticed that Dozei was not as quick as the others, and she frowned at the sorrel. For the last week, he had been favoring his off rear hoof. She decided that she would have to ask Himic to look at it, in case there was some damage. "Come, you four," she said, flicking the traces so that the team went from a trot to a canter. The transition was not smooth, and she knew that Himic would not be pleased. "I know!" she called out, forestalling his criticism.

"Then do something about it," he shouted back, raising his arms to encourage her as she swept by him. "Make them work!"

"They *are* working!" Tishtry shouted back. She set her jaw and tightened her hold on the traces. It infuriated her when anyone criticized her horses, and it was maddening to be treated like a beginner, knowing nothing about handling a team. She had been driving and riding horses for as long as she could remember, so she knew that she was better than almost anyone she had seen perform so far. "Dozei. Up!" she shouted as the sorrel lagged again. She used the traces to guide the team more tightly, holding them under firmer control than she usually did. Then she brought her team to a walk. She made sure her balance was perfect before taking them through their paces again: walk, trot, rack, canter, and gallop, striving to keep them absolutely in unison. This time they did better, and she began to relax, permitting herself to smile as she reined them down from gallop to walk. She halted them a few strides away from Himic and waited, keeping her team in perfect order as her aurigatore looked them over.

"Not too bad. You're going to have to train them to stand together, but that time you showed real improvement," he said after he had studied the way she held her team. "It'll make your stunts easier, too, once you've got them out of their bad habits. Now, I want you to take them on the lunge, all four of them, and get them used to moving together at your order. The Romans expect that of trick riders, and if the horses do not perform well—and a team like this one especially—they'll discount anything the rider can do."

149

A month ago, Tishtry would have argued with him, but now she accepted what he said with resignation. "All right; I'll work them four abreast on the lunge. Anything else?"

"You're going to have to learn to hold them tightly together. I want you to be able to put the chariot through those gates quickly and with room to spare. After that, we'll add a few new tricks to your repertoire." He favored her with a thumbs-up signal. "You're doing very well, and so I'll tell our master."

"Well, that's something," she said with an exaggerated show of relief. "I was beginning to fear I would never live up to your expectations."

He shook his head. "You haven't done so yet, but you're getting closer all the time," Himic said calmly. "You're not prepared for Roma, but by this time next year, no doubt you'll—"

"Next *year*?" Tishtry challenged him. "It won't take that long."

"It might," Himic said, refusing to dispute the matter with her. "I want you to have Petros massage you after you've had your bath: you're tense and that's affecting your driving. You can't afford to be tense when you're trying to hold four horses galloping flat out."

Tishtry could not disagree. "All right. But I want to spend more time doing my own tricks. You haven't let me do one handstand this week, and I'm afraid I'll get weak."

"All right. Tomorrow, if you can get your team to move in unison, you can do four somersaults and a handstand as a reward. Will that satisfy you?" He offered her a hand down from the chariot.

"No, but if that's the best you can do, I suppose I must endure it." She tossed her head saucily and came to take the reins from his hand.

"Incorrigible imp," he said, and made no attempt to mask the pride he felt in her.

The senior groom came out of Dozei's stall and motioned to Tishtry and Himic. "Well, I've had a look at his foot, and I must admit I don't like the look of it. You were right to call me in."

"What's the matter?" Tishtry asked. She glanced toward the sorrel, worry making her face appear much older.

"There's a weakness in the off rear pastern joint. He's favoring the hoof, no doubt about it, and it is not as flexible as it should be." He pursed his lips. "I'm going to suggest that his foot be soaked in hot water and that a poultice of mustard and egg white be applied to it every morning and every night for the next ten days. He should be ridden, too, but not drilled, and it would be better if he ran on grass instead of sand or bare earth. In time his leg may improve, but do not hold out hope for it." He hooked his thumbs into his belt. "He is valuable enough while he races, but if he cannot run well, your master must replace him and you will not have much money to buy another horse."

Himic interrupted this discouraging news. "Our master will replace the horse in her team and will provide her with a fifth one as well, so that if any of the others is harmed, she can continue to perform."

This surprised Tishtry, who had been trying to find a way to suggest adding another horse to her stable for more than a week. "When did he decide this?" she asked, paying little attention to the head groom.

"When he bought you. The question was how advanced you would become, and so Calpurnius has hesitated on the purchase until you are ready to stipulate the sort of animal you are capable of handling." He looked back at the head groom. "What of the sorrel: do you think he will improve in time?"

"Candidly?" the man asked. "With care, I think he will get better, but I doubt if he will ever again be able to work in the arena with the team. The leg has been damaged, and there is nothing I can do or say that will change it." He looked at Tishtry in a thoughtful way. "I am sorry to tell you this, girl, but you must face it sooner or later, and your master would prefer it be sooner, I think."

Tishtry nodded. "Yes, and it may be best for the team. I don't want the other three to fall into bad habits because of Dozei. The team is used to him, though, and new horses will be a problem as well." She went to the stall and reached over the gate to pat Dozei's rump. "He's a good fellow."

Dozei gave a rumbling whicker and raised his head a bit, though he seemed to be unhappy.

"You have handled him well, girl," the head groom assured her. "It is largely a matter of fortune and breeding with these horses. Some last longer when everyone expects them to collapse after one season; others that you would think would go on for years cannot sustain more than a few turns around the sands before they are useless to everyone."

"That's true enough," Himic agreed. "I had one horse,

a black-nosed gray. To look at him, you would have thought him incapable of pulling anything heavier than a child's cart. But with my quadriga, he pulled the rest of the team through more trouble than any animal I have owned before or since. A big ugly brute he was, with a head like a bucket and sloping shoulders that made you wonder how you'd keep a yoke on him for more than an hour. He had more stamina than any other horse I've owned."

Tishtry sensed that the two men were doing what they could to make her burden easier, and it gave her the first sense of friendship she had experienced since she had been through the storm with Holik. "Dozei is a good horse, but it is unwise to force him to perform if it hurts him and gives the team bad habits. It is best to take him out of the arena while he has worth enough to merit keeping him."

"Yes," Himic said, more in approval of her decision than seconding what she said. "I will arrange for him to be pastured here, so that the team will not be broken at once. It is always awkward when there have been just the four horses together for some time. You are used to what they do, and they are used to one another. Having a fifth horse will be an improvement."

The head groom coughed diplomatically. "You understand that the master might ask you to sell your sorrel if he would prefer not to pay for his keep."

"I know it's possible," Tishtry said carefully, already anticipating the arguments she would have to use to avoid that eventuality. "He is my horse, and if it is required, I suppose I can afford the payments if it comes to that." It would take funds from her savings to free

153

her family, but her horse was almost as important to her. She did her best to turn her thoughts from the disappointment her father would feel if he learned of her predicament.

"The new horses will make it easier," Himic said. "You may change your mind after you've developed the new team." He put his hand on Tishtry's shoulder as they walked out of the stables. "Dozei is a good horse. You taught him well and you have done nothing to abuse him. Some horses last longer than others. You know this, Tishtry."

She stared away from him. "I know it, yes. I had hoped that I wouldn't be in this situation for a while. And since I'm not performing just now, the expenses trouble me." She did not confide her fear that Calpurnius might grow tired of paying for her, and sell her just to be rid of the cost of keeping her and her horses.

Himic apparently understood her worry. "You are a great asset to Calpurnius. He is willing to wait a bit for your finest performances. Until now, your old master took advantage of your immediate skills, never thinking that in time, you would need to develop more of your abilities in order to increase your value. He never understood that aspect of owning an arena slave. He sought to enrich himself without any risk, and for that he was prepared to hold you back. Calpurnius is not like that. And," he added more thoughtfully, "you should be aware, girl, that in time, when you have become far more valuable, he will look to sell you. It is not his way to keep performers like you. He is willing to train you and to send you to more competitive amphitheaters, but he is not willing to keep you once you have realized your worth. I have seen him do this many times, and I know it will be the same with you."

Tishtry heard this out with more alarm than she wished to admit. In vain she told herself that being sold was the lot of all slaves, and that if Calpurnius used her wisely, she could benefit from it as much as he did. In her heart she felt the same betrayal that she had when Barantosz had sold her. She swallowed hard. "Then I pray the gods he will not part with me too soon, so that I will bring him the profit of my training."

With a slight, sad smile, Himic nodded. "Good girl."

"What do you think of them?" Calpurnius asked as Tishtry completed her first inspection of the two new horses.

She could not admit she was very pleased. "The black—Neronis? is that his name?—needs to lengthen his stride, but that red roan is splendid." She gave this second horse an affectionate slap on his flank. "Tehouti, that's what he's called."

"My purchasing agent had full records on your team, their size and strides, and he did everything he could to match them." Calpurnius braced his arms on the top rail of the practice ring. "Himic tells me that in another month you'll be ready to go back into the arena. What do you think?"

"I'd be willing to go today, but with new horses, I don't dare." She swung up and over the fence with practiced ease. "And there is an arena slave, a bestiarii whom Himic says I must see. Some Greek fellow, I understand. He has a team of dancing horses, they tell me." She sounded skeptical, but secretly was very curious. How could horses be made to dance? And if they could be made to dance, was it something that her own team should learn to do?

"That would be Dionysos. Aegidius Modestinus Valericus owns him, and has had great success with him. He has been performing in Patavium for several months, and Valericus recently decided to bring him here." Calpurnius looked at the red and black horses in the practice ring. "Himic tells me that they have very good feet and strong legs. That should stand for something."

"I hope," Tishtry said, then knew what was expected of her. "You were most generous, my master, to provide these new horses, and I am grateful that you gave them to me."

Calpurnius shrugged. "With the sort of performing you do, they would not be much use to anyone else in any case. I fully expect to be handsomely repaid for your team in the revenue you bring from your winnings and your performance fees." He started away from the ring, signaling Tishtry to come with him. "I have accepted a commission for your appearance in ten days. Do you think you can be ready by then? Himic has informed me that you have improved your performance, but that does not mean you're prepared to show the world."

"I'm willing," Tishtry said promptly, wondering where this was leading.

"I trust this is true, for there are many side bets being placed on you, and I stand to make a tidy sum if you justify my faith in you. Do you have at least six new tricks to perform in the arena?"

"Seven, in fact," she said proudly. "One of them is

very dangerous, and Himic has helped me find a way to make it even more spectacular than it is." She had to trot to keep up with him, for he not only walked swiftly, but was more than a head taller than she. "I spring off Immit's back, do a double backward somersault and land on my feet in the quadriga."

"Truly?" Calpurnius had stopped walking and stared at her. "Are you sure you will not be hurt?"

"No," she said. "But I have done it more than twenty times without mishap, and I am as confident as I can be that it will go precisely as I have practiced it." She did her best to appear unconcerned with the risk. "If the team were to shy, or I was to trip, or the quadriga hit something in the sand, then I might be injured, but such things happen rarely."

"I'll talk to Himic about this," Calpurnius told her, his mouth setting in a stern line.

"Yes; do. He knows better than I do how well I perform it." She braced her hands on her hips. "In another half year, I will be able to do better than that. I am certain of it."

CHAPTER
XIV

Dionysos gave a signal and his ten horses rose on their hind legs together, first turning to the left, then the right. The one on the end, a clay-colored stallion from Gaul, moved ahead of the rest, hopping on his rear feet with every snap of Dionysos' whip. At another sign, the horses dropped back to all fours, and began a slow rack in an interlocking loop pattern.

"They're wonderful," Tishtry sighed to Himic as she watched the performance. "They make my team look like dray beasts."

"Oh, it's not that bad, surely," Himic said, attempting to reassure her.

"You wait. That is what the crowd will think, and who can blame them?" She leaned her forehead on her hand. "Calpurnius will sell me for sure, and I'll end up mucking out stalls in Tingis or Olbia, or some other remote end of the Empire, and I'll have to sell my horses and I'll never get my family's freedom.''

''He's good, but he's not that good,'' Himic said more bracingly. ''He can't ride anywhere near as well as you do, and that ridiculous double-rank-of-five hitch of his is about as maneuverable as an oxcart.''

''But look what his horses can do,'' she wailed softly. ''Even at his very, very best, Shirdas can't do half of what that tan stallion of his does.''

''Then perhaps you should think of teaching your team a few more tricks,'' Himic suggested, careful to make it sound as if he did not expect this of her.

''Perhaps,'' she echoed morosely. ''And look at Dionysos himself! He's like one of those Greek statues, with a profile that must drive every woman under fifty to distraction.'' She made her hands into fists. ''Golden curls, huge blue eyes, and his tunica dyed to match his eyes. Valericus must be overjoyed to have such a slave as that.''

''Calpurnius is pleased to have you,'' Himic reminded her, trying to encourage her. ''And you may not be a work of art like that youngster—''

''I look a complete barbarian beside him,'' she corrected Himic sharply. ''There is no need to flatter me. I know that I am no beauty, and even if I were, I would have to look better than Aphrodite to compare with that Apollo there.''

''The Emperor has blond curls and blue eyes, too, and though he is handsome enough, he is nothing to rival Dionysos. That may be why Valericus is reluctant to take him to Roma, for fear the Emperor would be offended." Himic laughed quietly. "It will take a great deal of cleverness on Valericus' part not to offend Nero with that glorious youth."

Tishtry cocked her head to the side. "Why?"

"Because Nero does not like to have any who rival him, and believe me, that slave would cast the Emperor into the shade. Valericus must arrange it so that Nero himself orders Dionysos to the Circus Maximus, or he will find himself in great disfavor."

"Well, Nero certainly has nothing to fear from me," Tishtry said wryly. "Unless the Romans are mad for squat women with clubbed hair."

Himic patted her shoulder. "Very good, Tishtry. You are learning a little wisdom at last. Beauty is a great danger for slaves. Remember that."

"What reason have I to remember it?" Tishtry asked wistfully.

"Not for yourself, perhaps, but for others. In time you will be grateful that you need concern yourself with little more than your performing skills. There are many others who would gladly trade with you." He studied the golden curls that Dionysos took such obvious pride in. "Slaves are not permitted to refuse the claims of their masters, or those their masters favor. With one as beautiful as that Greek boy, Valericus would be a fool not to take advantage of Dionysos' good looks, and Dionysos will have no opportunity to accept or refuse the attentions his master permits. I doubt you wish to live that way, Tishtry."

She was frowning as she listened. "No," she said at last. "I would not like to be my master's plaything. But

160

there are slaves who earn their freedom in catering to their masters' wants."

"Wouldn't you rather buy your freedom through your own abilities?" Himic asked gently.

Tishtry could not help smiling. "Yes."

"Then don't look at him with so much envy," Himic ordered.

"Can't I envy his horses?" Tishtry protested.

"Only if you believe you cannot do better yourself," he responded, chucking her on the jaw as they watched Dionysos acknowledge the applause of the crowd.

"Where are you from? Your Greek is terrible." Dionysos regarded Tishtry arrogantly as she prepared to enter the arena.

"I'm Armenian. My first master comes from near Satala in Cappadocia," she answered, trying not to mimic his tone.

"By Poseidon, that is the end of the world. No wonder you are so lacking in graces." He bowed to her with a condescending smile.

"Yes, we have not yet had the chance to become effete," she agreed with sweet malice just before she gave the sign to Himic to release her team so that she could rush through the Gates of Life onto the sands. She could feel her face redden because of the insult Dionysos had given her, and her swipe had not given her enough satisfaction to make up for what he had said. She knew that he had intended to rattle her so that she would not perform well on this first appearance in the arena in several months, and that alone gave her

161

the necessary will to concentrate on her performance. She braced her feet in the special racing chariot Calpurnius had provided her and slapped the traces over her team's backs. She refused to permit that smug, conceited Greek any more enjoyment at her expense.

She heard the welcoming roar of voices, and she took her team around the arena once, holding them to their perfectly matched trot every step of the way. Neronis was yoked up in Dozei's place, but by now the horses were used to each other. She felt her nervousness melt away as she began her performance, moving from the chariot onto Immit's back. As the team stretched into a canter, Tishtry raised her head and flashed a smile at the stands.

Her first two new tricks brought hoots of approval from her audience: while standing on her hands, she walked from the back of Shirdas, to Immit, to Neronis, to Amath, then ended with a backflip that carried her to Shirdas again. Here she paused long enough to get her breath, then she grabbed a handful of Shirdas' mane and swung under his neck to Immit. Here she reached for the mare's mane, then vaulted onto Immit's back, and repeated the loop under Neronis' neck and onto Amath's back. The drumming of their hooves was louder than the shouts of approval from her audience, and Tishtry was a little startled to see that some of the crowd were throwing blossoms into the arena in appreciation of her new stunts. She returned to her old routine for a bit, then did the splits across the backs on her running team. This brought another wave of shouts and a fresh shower of blossoms.

When Tishtry finally did her back spring with the

double somersault that ended with her standing once again in her quadriga, the ovation was staggering. In all her years, she had never heard anything like it for a bestiarii. Usually such enthusiasm was reserved for gladiators and other fighters. She brought her team to the front of the editor's box, where her team dipped their heads to the man who was sponsoring the Games that day, which evoked a little more tumult from the crowd.

"Most worthy!" the editor shouted in order to be heard at all.

"For the glory of my master and the gods," Tishtry replied, as was proper. Then she wheeled her team and set them at a smart trot for the Gates of Life. As she left the arena, she saw Dionysos' face, contorted with disgust and fury, watching her from the shadows by the Master of the Bestiarii's shed.

Calpurnius was beaming as he came up to Tishtry that evening. "You surpassed everything," he said grandly, and Tishtry could tell that he was slightly drunk. "I won over twelve thousand denarii on bets alone, and your performance fee has gone up by two hundred denarii. Here." He held out a small pouch in which coins clinked. "For all you did. Add it to your account to buy your family's freedom. There will be more soon if you continue as you have performed today." His smile became silly. "They were all agog over that Greek, and no one thought you'd have anything new to offer, but you showed them, didn't you? Valericus has already offered quite a lot of money for you, but I've refused him. In six months, I'll be able to name the amount and anyone who is able will think himself lucky to get you."

"So soon?" Tishtry asked in spite of herself.

"Maybe a year," Calpurnius allowed. "But you're improving so much, and your style has become so polished that everyone is mad for you." He noticed that one end of his toga had come loose and he held it out, puzzling what to do with it. "You will race again in ten days. Not an hour before. We can't go spoiling your effectiveness with too many performances, can we? You are rare, girl, and I intend that you should stay that way. Valericus has his Greek in the arena four times in the next ten days, and by then some of the crowd will be used to him, and they will not think anything of watching him make his horses dance. But you, they will be waiting for you so eagerly." He rubbed his hands together and more of his toga trailed on the ground. "Valericus will be furious, of course, but by then it will be too late."

Tishtry, who was feeling more exhausted than she cared to admit, looked at her master with curiosity. "Is it your intention to create a rivalry between me and Dionysos?"

"I don't need to," he answered with glee. "It already exists. There are men betting that the Greek will not be able to do more than drive his chariot, and will not be able to stand on his team's backs, let alone do somersaults and handstands and all the rest of it. How do you keep from getting trampled when you go under the necks that way?" he asked suddenly.

"It takes a great deal of practice," she answered, not adding that if she were much larger, she would not be able to do it at all. "You are very near the legs when you swing under the neck, you know."

"Um," he responded owlishly. "I wouldn't like to try it, myself."

"It requires training, both for you and the horses," she said, hoping that Calpurnius would not decide to attempt it.

"Well, I know my horses wouldn't put up with it, even standing still." He gathered up the end of his toga and knotted it—very incorrectly—around his waist. "Terrible garment. You'd think they'd let us wear something sensible to a banquet, like a tunica or a dalmatica, but no, men of rank must have on the toga, or they will be thought boors. It shows you what fools we are." He leaned back against the stable wall and stared off into the twilight for some little time, saying nothing to Tishtry.

When she had waited for some more response and none came, she took one step back, assuming he would dismiss her. "Master?"

"No, no. I'm not through yet. I'm thinking." He cleared his throat. "You truly dislike that Greek, don't you?"

She hesitated, then answered directly. "I dislike his manners, and it appears that he dislikes mine. Beyond that, I don't know. He has not spoken much to me, nor I to him." It would be improper of her to say more unless Calpurnius ordered her to elaborate.

"Would you like to meet him in some kind of challenge demonstration?" There was a greediness in his eyes that startled Tishtry.

"It would depend on the circumstances and conditions. Clearly his team can outperform mine by most

165

standards, but just as clearly, I can outperform *him* by most standards. You would have to take that into consideration if there were to be such a demonstration." She watched him, trying to think of some way to caution him. "I doubt any conditions could be made that both of us would think fair."

"That doesn't matter," Calpurnius said, dismissing her reservations. "Valericus is itching to take advantage of the situation, and so am I." He stared off into nothing for a bit. "Well," he went on as if there had been no lapse, "I will consider this all very carefully, you may be sure of that. I'll talk to Himic, too, and find out what he thinks. We could all realize great profits from a contest between the two of you, should you win. And I expect you to win if we make such an arrangement."

"Valericus will expect Dionysos to win, as well," Tishtry reminded her master. "They will not be willing to have such a match otherwise."

"Naturally," Calpurnius chortled. "That is what makes it so delicious. You said yourself that you can outride him, and I know that you can get through tighter spots than his team can, and if it comes down to hard cases, the bestiarii is more important than the beasts."

"Not according to the ones who work with lions and tigers," Tishtry said, beginning to feel seriously alarmed.

"I've already talked to a chariot maker. There's a radical new design being tried out, one in which the tongue has a certain amount of swivel, so that the chariots can make tighter turns. I hear the traders on the Silk Road use wagons with hinged tongues like this, so that they can manage all the twists and turns of the mountain roads. Think of the advantage that could be for someone like you." He regarded Tishtry expectantly. "What do you say? Does it intrigue you?"

"I will have to see the chariot first," she said gently. "Once I know what the chariot maker has in mind, then I will be able to say more. I might be overjoyed, but it is possible that the modification will not be satisfactory." She wanted so much to talk to Himic and find out what he thought of all this. "And I don't know that my team will adapt well to it. We will have to wait and see."

"All right." He looked a bit sulky. "You're right, I suppose. But we can make a lot, you and Himic and I, if we can pull this off. A win in a demonstration against Dionysos and you will be the most sought-after bestiarii this side of Roma. You can buy the freedom of a dozen families, if you wish, and you can take yourself back to Armenia a freedwoman, if that would please you."

Tishtry hardly believed what he told her. "I want to perform awhile," she stammered, realizing that it was true.

"Well, you think about it. I'll want to see you in the morning, and you can come with me to the chariot maker." He waggled his fingers at her and ambled off, humming the melody of "Jupiter, the Biggest and Best" as he went.

When Calpurnius was gone, Tishtry went back to her quarters, trying to gather her thoughts. Suppose she did accept the challenge and suppose she did win the contest, and suppose there were winnings of the sort that Calpurnius suggested there might be, what then? She had known from her youth that she would one day buy her family's freedom, and had worked toward that goal with diligence. But her own freedom was another matter. Would she buy it now, if she could? And what would she have if she did? Two chariots, five horses, three sets of clothing, and a handful of coins. With that, she could return to her family, but what then? Would she be content to raise and train a few horses for a provincial charioteer to drive? She had to admit that was no longer enough for her. She wanted to drive in Roma, to perform for Nero, perhaps, and hear the cheers of the thousands in the stands of the Circus Maximus. When she retired, she would buy her freedom, and it would be on her own terms, to be the most sought-after trainer of young stunt drivers in the entire Empire. She would not have to live at the back of the world and scrape by like a peasant, but would be able to afford a villa and good breeding stock. Perhaps she would bring her family to be with her then. That made her laugh, and for the first time in months she slept with a smile on her face.

CHAPTER

Himic pulled Tishtry aside and asked in an undervoice, "What do you think of the chariot? Balancing in it will be very difficult—much harder than it is in your racing quadriga. Those leaps and flips of yours might overturn it when you land in the chariot."

"It's possible," Tishtry agreed. "But think of how maneuverable it is. I could run the whole team on neck harnesses and traces instead of yoking the outer three horses, and that would mean more flexibility. I have to find some advantage to offset the abilities of the Greek's horses." It was a good, sensible argument, and they both knew it.

"You're willing to accept the risks, then? Because the risks are genuine and you would be unwise to deny them." He frowned at her. "I can dissuade our master if that would be the best course. He knows that my experience outweighs his enthusiasms." With a sigh, he added, "I know *I* wouldn't want to perform in one of those things."

"But you're not a stunt charioteer, you were a racing charioteer," Tishtry reminded him. "There's a world of difference in that." She cocked her head. "You know, if I could put those light saddles on my team—the little ones I showed you, with the fenders on them for hand-stands and other stunts—and the neck harnesses, I would be able to do even more stunts while taking the team through tighter maneuvers. What do you think?"

"I think it's very dangerous," Himic said.

"Well, most stunts are. But if I don't find that kind of advantage, I'll clearly not be able to come out with a victory the way our master intends I should. I need to have at least one stunt that is beyond anything the Greek has ever done and ever will do."

"Possibly," Himic grumbled. "It's also possible that you'll be hurt or your horses injured with a vehicle like that, and what then?"

"That could happen at any time," Tishtry said as nonchalantly as she could. "You know what the arena is like. Those of us who perform there get hurt every day."

"Yes; I limp," Himic agreed. "You'll have to think about this carefully, girl, before you let our master go through with it. You have more to lose than he does."

"What could stop him now?" She looked at him. "Well? You say he'll listen to you, but he's more excited than I've known him to be in the past. Perhaps he's been this way with you, but I warrant it wasn't often, was it?" She could tell from his expression that Calpurnius was rarely so set upon a contest as he was now. "Himic, you know our master. If I disappoint him now, he won't take it kindly. Both of us could suffer more for refusing than accepting. If I have an accident, then it is the will of the gods and no one can be blamed. But if I say I will not race against Dionysos, it will be thought that the Greek truly is superior, or that I was bribed to refuse, and either way, my advancement stops here."

"You're ambitious, girl," Himic said, and made it a warning.

"Yes, and anyone in my position would be." She looked back at the chariot. "If I have six weeks to practice, I think I can develop a means to handle the thing, for that one contest, at least. And I will want to find a way to keep the team on neck harnesses, which that chariot will permit. That way, if I have to, I can release each horse individually. The way Dionysos has his team trained, I had better find the means to give my horses a bit more liberty, or he will be able to force my horses to break pace, and that could be disastrous for me."

"All right," Himic said with a shake of his head. "But I do not want you to make rash promises to Calpurnius. Let me be the one to negotiate the terms of the contest, not you. You're rash enough to give away advantages that you very much need." He saw Calpurnius gesture to him. "I have to talk with him now. You wait here. I'll inform him you will abide by my decision, since I have the greater arena experience. And you will *not* dispute that, will you?"

"No," Tishtry said, and did as he told her, relieved that she would not have to argue directly with Calpurnius. She rubbed her hands together and noticed that they were wet. It troubled her to see that she had become so worried about the upcoming contest.

"Well, it is all arranged," Calpurnius informed her a week later. "I have just had confirmation from Valericus, and the Master of the Bestiarii has agreed to permit your contest to be the first in the day, so that there will be no blood on the sands to distract your horses. You will meet in two months, at the beginning of the three days of Games. Valericus and I will be joint editoris of the Games, with the approval of the Senate. You will be the first event, and the last will be a great venation, with ten kinds of animals and three kinds of hunters, including pygmies from Africa. We are already placing orders for animals. We have arranged also for a second chariot competition for bestiarii, in this case, five chariots, each drawn by different sorts of beasts. I have been told that Nero himself delights in these competitions. There will be leopards and bears and ostriches and wild pigs and wolves, the whole to be refereed by two men riding rhinoceroses. Nothing like it has been done here before, and everyone will talk of it. My reputation will increase and yours will be made throughout the Empire." He looked up from his writing table. "Does that please you, girl?"

"I hope it will, when it is over," she answered.

"I am presenting you with the new chariot we discussed. It will be delivered the day after tomorrow, and I will expect you to work with it hourly. Himic has been given his instructions." He stopped and looked at her with uncharacteristic directness. "You must win for me, girl. I am on the brink of ruin, and if this does not prosper, there will be nothing left."

This stark admission amazed Tishtry. "I . . . I don't understand," she said when it became apparent that she had to say something.

"I have almost nothing left. This contest of yours, these Games, are my last chance to succeed. Between what I will realize from your winning and the price I will be able to ask for you afterward, my House will be saved. You think you are the only one in the world trying to buy your family's freedom? I admit that mine do not wear collars, but if you fail, we are all as good as slaves." He put down the paper he had been reading. "I do not want to threaten you, girl, but make no doubt about it: you must win."

Tishtry nodded. "I always do the best I am able to do," she said stiffly, still trying to sort out what Calpurnius had told her.

"It has to be better than that," he said. "You must give the performance of your life. There must be no question that you triumph entirely over that too-pretty Greek of Valericus'. Do you understand me?"

"I believe I do," she said unhappily. "And I still tell you that I always do the best that I can." She coughed to try to ease the tension in her throat. "I . . . I was not aware that these Games were so crucial."

"Now you are. That is why I have told you all this." He stared at the paper. "This is the outlining of terms from Valericus. I have affixed my signature and my seal to it, and we have been informed that the Senate will not withhold its approval. Tonight I am going to write to my father and inform him of what I have done. It is my intention to promise him success. Can you tell me any reason that I should not do this? Can you?"

"No," she said softly.

"Remember everything I've said, when you are offered bribes, and when you see Himic inspecting your chariot and tack. You must be very careful now, for I am not the only man whose fortune rides with you. The courts would not call it slave abuse if I beat you for losing such an encounter. Keep that in mind."

"I will." She wondered if he could hear her heart battering at her ribs, and decided that he was not paying enough attention to notice. She could feel color mount in her face, which only made her embarrassment worse.

"If you bring me honor and fortune, you will have all the money I have promised you, and I will see that you are sold to the greatest advantage possible. That will mean success for you. Your value is increasing— you are already worth twice what I paid for you—and if you win against the Greek, you will be the most valuable performer I have ever owned. I will see that you bring every denarius you are worth when I sell you, you have my word on that, and I will say this to my father, so that he will know of it as well, and will testify to it if the Senate requires it of him. You may take your case to any court in the Empire if you doubt I have done well by you, and it will see that your wrongs are redressed. If you win. If you win."

"Yes; if I win," she repeated.

"Your fortunes are in your hands as well as my fortunes. Do not forget that." He rolled the paper up and secured it with a ribbon. "My majordomo will take this back to Valericus tonight. The Games are set. The contest is accepted. All right?"

"Yes," she whispered, her mouth very dry.

"And you understand what I have told you?" He tapped the table with his signet. "Do you?"

"Yes."

"Then it is set," he said, clapping his hands to summon his majordomo. "For Valericus, and for the sake of Mercury and Mars, be sure to mind the footman when you step across the threshold. You must enter the house on the right foot. Be sure you do. We need no ill omens attending this competition."

The majordomo, an angular old Greek, took the scroll from his master with great dignity. "It will be precisely as you wish," he said in elegant Latin, then, with a look that completely ignored Tishtry, he left the room.

"I am depending on you, girl," Calpurnius said softly. "My House is depending on you, just as your family is. Never forget that."

"I won't," Tishtry promised, and fled the place as soon as Calpurnius made the gesture that dismissed her.

For the two days she waited for the new chariot, she worked her horses with light practice bigae, substituting little stunt saddles and neck harnesses for the more usual three-horse yokes with the inside horse on neck harness. Having just two horses to handle instead of four made it easier to get them used to the new tack, and it gave Tishtry the opportunity to lose herself in exercise. Any moment that she was not busy, she fretted as piercingly clear memories of her interview with Calpurnius returned to her. The overwhelming responsibility her master had placed on her shoulders caused her so much anxiety that she could not sleep unless she was so exhausted that she could hardly move.

"You aren't eating properly," Himic chided her the morning the new chariot arrived. "I've been watching you, and you have not finished one meal since the contract for these Games was signed."

"With a lighter chariot, I should be lighter as well," she said shortly.

"Nonsense. You need all the strength you can get to be able to hold that thing without tipping it over." Himic stuck his thumbs through his belt. "You better tell me what it is, or you'll be in pieces long before you enter the arena for the contest."

Calpurnius had not told Tishtry to keep silent, but she was reluctant to tell Himic, for fear that gossip would make the contest even more hazardous than it already was. She hesitated, trying to think of a way to account for her nerves that would not entail discussing their owner. "I have never been challenged this way before, and I'm troubled by it."

"You weren't earlier," Himic said, doubt in his expression and his voice.

"The contract had not been signed," she said.

"You've never turned edgy with previous contracts," he said, more skeptically than before.

"They weren't on such a scale as this one," she said, getting up from her place on the tack room bench. "This is a very major contest, not simply a demonstration of what I can do with my team and the gear my sister made for me." As she said that, she missed Macon so fiercely that she thought she might cry.

"Sorry, girl, but it's not good enough. Something has spooked you and you're acting as if the fate of the Empire is at stake in your contest." He must have seen some change in her, for he took her by the shoulder. "What *is* it? What has happened to you? Were you threatened?"

"Not . . . that way," she said slowly. "Not the way you mean."

"I don't mean any way," Himic insisted. "I don't care who threatened you, or what the threat was, you tell our master about it, and he'll be sure that something is done—" He stopped. "Oh. Calpurnius threatened, did he?"

"I didn't say that!" Tishtry protested, trying to get away from the old charioteer.

"You didn't have to," Himic said reasonably, shoving her back down onto the bench. "What's he done, gone and bet his last denarius on the contest?" He nodded when Tishtry said nothing. "He never learns. It was gambling that got him sent here, and he's still at it." He sat on the bench beside her. "What does he expect you to do?"

"To win," Tishtry said miserably.

"Well, that's understandable. I expect it of you, as well." He put his arm around her shoulder. "What are the stakes?"

"He says everything—his fortune, the fortune of his House—and it must be a clear victory. Then he will give me money and sell me well and he will be out of danger." She hung her head. "He said that I could free his family as well as my own."

Himic shook his head sadly. "You must do the best you can. You always do that. But for the rest, no matter what you do, I think that Calpurnius intends to sell you after the Games. He will make as much money as he can, and *that* is where he stands to gain the most, not through betting. For one thing, he doesn't have that much money anymore. Oh, he has this villa and his slaves and a few other things, but he is not as rich as he pretends to be, and his greatest asset is the four arena slaves he owns."

"What will happen, then? Will he give me money for winning so I can buy my family's freedom, or was that . . ." She could not bring herself to accuse her master of lying, though it was precisely what she thought.

"If you win, he will undoubtedly give you something, but don't expect it to be much." He paused, considering what more he ought to say. "You've got to understand that Calpurnius has a reputation for finding very promising youngsters."

"Like me?" she asked with a bitterness that was more surprising to her than to Himic.

"Yes. You're one of the best, because you came here with more experience than most bestiarii your age have, and you are able to do things the others cannot, and will probably never be able to do." He paused, so that she would have a chance to ask him questions if that was what she wanted to do, but she remained silent. "There is another side to this that you haven't considered yet, girl."

"What's that?" she muttered.

"Calpurnius does have a reputation, as I have told you. Which means that there are many who respect his judgment and who will come to see what new treasure he has found. It means that you could be sold to your advantage as much as to Calpurnius'. You have said you want to perform in Roma—little though you may believe it now, you may get that chance through this contest coming up. And do not permit Calpurnius to burden you as he has. I will speak to him myself, but if he tries to bludgeon you again with so much responsibility, then you must tell him that you do not perform well when you are greatly worried. That will make him stop at once."

In spite of her mood, Tishtry let a watery chuckle escape her. "He wouldn't like that, would he?"

"Not at all." He got to his feet. "Another thing: if he tries to find reasons to punish you, or threatens you with retribution for losing, remind him that the magistrates would levy a fine on him for abuse of a willing slave. That will also make him stop and think."

Tishtry looked up at him. "Would the magistrates truly do that?"

"Yes. Calpurnius has done it before, and there are those who would testify that you are honorable in competition. Don't forget, girl, that the Romans had a slave rebellion not so long ago, and they do not want another one. They know that slaves who do not have to suffer abuse are not as likely to rebel, and that slaves with recourse to law will not resort to violence." He held out his hand to Tishtry. "Come on, girl. We'd better go have a look at your horses' hooves."

Tishtry accepted his hand, her mind less troubled

179

now. "All right. And I want to get some more of that paste with wool fat and ground seaweed. We had best take extra care of the team just now; if we're going to win, they must stay in perfect shape."

CHAPTER

XVI

Two days before the race, Himic found an unfamiliar slave attempting to get into the stables where Calpurnius' slaves kept their teams. He claimed that he had been sent to deliver new traces, but Tishtry said she had not ordered and did not want new traces. The slave was sent away with a warning, but Himic would not let the matter rest.

"There is a great deal of money being bet, and you are the one who should be most careful." He gave Tishtry a long, hard look. "We're going to need guards. We should have had them before now, but Calpurnius has not wanted to spend the money for them. Once I tell him about this incident, however—"

"What incident?" Tishtry asked. "The man was probably nothing more than a spy for Valericus."

"And if he were, what then?" Himic inquired. "Suppose he had carried a little knife, the kind that you might use to trim a hoof. It can also cut a tendon or lame a foot." He looked at the other grooms gathered at the entrance to the stable. "From now on, you must all be very careful, or it may go badly for all of us. It need not be anything so obvious as poison. A horse might be given extra salt, and then provided water. You know how badly a horse would run who had three extra pails of water inside him weighing him down. Just one horse in a team with such a problem would mean that all would run badly. Keep watch on the feed for the horses. In fact, Tishtry, you had better be the one to feed them. She is the only one to be allowed to feed her horses," Himic said to the grooms. "No one else. That includes any of you, and me, and our master, for that matter."

Tishtry listened, her mind on the coming contest. She felt that Himic was too cautious, but she also knew that it was better to be too cautious now than to regret a lack of caution later. She looked over the other grooms. "I think," she said when there was a break in Himic's instructions, "it would be best if I take care of cleaning the stalls and putting down the bedding straw, as well. The horses will like it and nothing will get into their stalls that should not."

"If you want to muck out your team's stalls, who are we to object?" one old groom called out, and the others laughed.

Himic quieted them with a gesture of his raised hands. "Tomorrow an old friend of mine is coming, and I will ask him if he has any suggestions. He has much experience of the Games, and he might know some things we should watch for." He waited a moment, then added, "There should be a guard on her chariot and tack every hour of the day and night."

"Isn't that a bit extreme?" Tishtry asked.

"No," Himic replied, and two of the grooms nodded in agreement. "In Roma, when a contest of this importance is approaching, they use officers of the Watch to guard the animals and the contestants, so that there can be no accusations later of sabotage."

Tishtry's smile showed her disbelief. "That's ridiculous," she told Himic, and looked to the grooms to agree with her.

"It's not," Himic said very seriously. "With as much money as this contest has involved with it, there are many who will do their best to influence the outcome one way or another." He looked at the grooms now. "We must be very careful, all of us. And if any one of you is found being lax, or taking bribes, Calpurnius will give you to the Emperor and you will spend your life sweating in the sandstone quarries in Egypt, or at the oar of a trireme. Betrayal of a master is a serious offense." Now he folded his arms, his attitude more severe than ever. "This is more serious than you know. When so much money is at risk, slaves must guard themselves."

One of the grooms looked up at the ceiling. "Slaves might also add to their riches."

"If you believe that, you will bring your own ruin, and the ruin of all of us. If you doubt that, speak to Caldos, the blink beggar by the Temple of Mars. Ask him how he came to be there." Himic turned to Tishtry.

"Tishtry, it is not right that you should not be protected as you ought to be, but since our master will do nothing, it is up to the rest of us to guard you."

"Guard me?" Tishtry laughed nervously, feeling genuinely frightened for the first time since Himic had started talking. "I don't think it's necessary to go so far. I'm careful and you're sensible."

"It may be that you won't need a guard, but if it is, we must be prepared." Plainly there was no changing his mind.

Another of the grooms stepped forward. "A man came to me yesterday, and said that he wanted to look at Tishtry's team. He said he wanted to see her horses up close before making his bets. He offered me money to see them."

Himic stiffened, and Tishtry could feel her features become fixed. It was Himic who spoke first. "What did you do?"

Tishtry held her breath, then made herself speak. "Yes. What did you do?"

"I said that he would have to talk to you, Himic. I said that I was not allowed into the stables where the racing horses are kept. But Himic, it was so much money." He paused again, then went on, still speaking with formality because of the seriousness of their discussion. "I might have done it, if he had offered me less, but that much money, just to look at horses, hardly seemed reasonable. I did not want to take so much."

The youngest groom laughed harshly. "Take the money. What is it to us if they want to gamble it away?"

Himic rounded on the young groom. "And what if the man had given her horses poison, or hurt them?

What if he had dropped a deadly serpent in the stalls, or put scorpions in their bedding? Do not think that is unlikely, for I have seen that and much worse done in the years when I still rode in the arena. Do not forget what these rivalries mean to the crowd, and to the men who own arena slaves." He looked at the men and then gave his attention to Tishtry once more. "I must tell Calpurnius about this. But you will not have to keep watch over your team unaided. I have a friend coming to observe the contest, and he will help you."

"Another former charioteer?" Tishtry asked suspiciously.

"Yes. His name is Lykos and he is eager to see you perform." That was all Himic was willing to say in front of the other grooms. He took Tishtry by the elbow and pulled her aside. "I must speak to these men in private, so that they will not be embarrassed to speak their minds. They are jealous of you, many of them, and what greed will not prompt them to do, spite could. I will have to determine that for myself, and I cannot do that while you are here."

"Why would they be spiteful?" Tishtry asked, amazed at the suggestion.

"You have accomplished more than they have, more than most of them ever could. You may well live to be free and to buy the freedom of your family, and some of those men envy you your opportunities. Some do not approve of what you do because among their peoples, women do not excel at the Games. Some dislike Armenians. There are many factors in jealousy, girl."

"And you?" Tishtry asked. "Are you jealous?"

"No, not very much. I have been in the arena, and

185

I have heard the crowd roar my name. Unlike you, I have no family, and it has been easier to remain a slave than to buy the uncertainties of freedom. The law requires that our master care for me and provide a reasonable life, and a place to live when I am too old and too lame to work anymore. I haven't your courage, and there are times I wish I did." He smiled sadly. "Go on. I have to tend to my duties here and you need to have time to think."

"Yes," she said quietly, and wandered off toward the grape arbor while Himic went back to speak to the grooms.

Lykos was tall and thin; his dalmatica was made of embroidered linen and his caligulae were of red leather and laced halfway up his legs. His hair had receded, leaving him with a curly white fringe around the shine of his pate. "It is good to meet you, girl," he said when Himic brought him across the practice arena to her side. "You handle your team like a veteran."

Tishtry bristled. "I *am* a veteran. I have been riding for more than ten years."

"And you are about fifteen," Lykos stated, not needing her to confirm this. "A very long time. But I have seen men twice your age who have been in the arena for twenty years who still cannot use their teams as well as you use yours." He had a way of smiling with his eyes that Tishtry liked. "So these are your horses. Why do you keep that lame sorrel in the ring with the others?"

"I have had Dozei from the first. The team is used to him." She pointed out the others. "Neronis and

Tehouti are new. The others I chose when my first master sent me to my first performances."

"Very good." He glanced at Himic. "You have not exaggerated, my old friend. What this girl can do is remarkable."

Over the years, Tishtry had come to hate being talked about as if she were not present. "I thank you," she snapped.

"No, no, girl," Lykos said at once. "Do not be offended. I had a discussion with Himic earlier today, and I had told him I reserved judgment until I saw for myself."

"Well, you haven't seen for yourself, not yet," Tishtry countered, not the least mollified. "You have only seen my team on the lunge, and you have no idea what I can do with them."

"On the contrary," Lykos said politely. "I do not have to see you do your stunts to know that you will do them well. That is obvious from the way you handle your team. Surely you are able to determine if a man is good on a horse simply by the way he walks up to one."

"Yes," she admitted grudgingly.

"Then assume I can tell you know your craft by the way you work your horses on the lunge." He stepped back. "Tomorrow is the demonstration race. I am very much looking forward to it."

"So am I," Tishtry said, feeling her excitement mounting as she spoke the words. Only the uncertainty of her future kept her from grinning with anticipation. "That Greek will have to have his team in better order than it has ever been if he intends to best me."

"Don't boast that way, girl; you tempt the gods," Himic warned her.

"The gods will do as they wish. I am more concerned about the things that men will be tempted to do." She put her hands on her hips. "Tonight, I will want another man to keep guard with me. I must sleep, and even if I sleep in the stables, there must be another to guard my horses."

Himic sighed. "I will be there for half the night." He turned to Lykos. "It is as you suspected—there are those who are trying to improve their odds."

"At Ancona we can order soldiers, of course, but here, Calpurnius would have to ask the garrison to loan you a few soldiers. There should be a better way. I have brought three men with me. They are trustworthy and they will not be bribed or battled." He looked at Tishtry. "Will you accept the loan of my men? They are used to guarding teams for the arena, and they will be as careful with your horses as they are with the best in the world."

For the first time, Tishtry wondered who this richly dressed slave was. "What men do you bring with you?"

"They work for me, and they do this duty regularly in our own arena." He gestured to Himic. "You have not told her?"

Himic shrugged. "Lykos is the Master of the Bestiarii at the Ancona amphitheater."

Tishtry stared. "The Master of the Bestiarii?" Lykos was a very powerful man, and his amphitheater was one of the most important in the Empire outside of Roma itself. "And you came here to see this contest?"

"Yes. And I must admit, not entirely innocently. I have been authorized to speak to your master on behalf of a man who wishes to buy you." He hesitated. "You are aware that Calpurnius intends to sell you."

"Yes. He said so." She looked down at her boots. "After the contest, he'll be able to set a price, or so he said."

Lykos touched her shoulder. "Do not let that prey on you."

"I try not to. It isn't always easy." She whistled for her team. "I have to rub them down and see them fed and watered and walked. Later tonight, while I change their bedding straw, perhaps we can talk then, if you are inclined to do so." She felt awkward making this suggestion, but she knew that she would have to talk to this impressive man sooner or later, and it might be easier before she raced than after.

"I will look forward to it. After I post my men, I will come to you." He motioned to Himic. "Come, old friend. I brought some wine with me that we should share, in memory of those old days in the arena."

Himic clapped his arm around Lykos' shoulders, and the two left Tishtry to her horses.

Her horses were fed a mixture of wheat, barley, oats, and millet, with nuts, raisins, and chopped apples mixed through it. Tishtry brushed them to a high gloss and coated their hooves with the mixture of wool fat and ground seaweed that Himic had given her. She inspected her horses' eyes and teeth and smelled their breath, to be sure they were as healthy as they could be. Then she left an old Thracian groom to watch them while she went off to have her evening meal.

Because she would not eat again until after the race, Calpurnius' cooks had provided a generous meal for her: ground pork in a spicy sauce served over bread chunks, followed by roasted chicken coated in honey and cinnamon. Then came vegetables cooked in milk with baked kid and a braised fish seasoned with liquamen; next, scallops wrapped in bacon and broiled. Last there were dates and figs in a mixture of wine and honey. Tishtry resisted the urge to eat quickly, and took her time with her supper, savoring the foods and enjoying the flavors of all of them. She had rarely had such a fine meal, and she did not know when she would have another such. Morosely, she told herself it would depend upon who bought her and what became of her next.

By the time she went back to the stables, Lykos was waiting for her. "I have heard that there is a great deal of betting going on about your contest."

"I have heard that, too," she said. "Calpurnius has told me that his whole fortune is at risk on these Games." She had not intended to sound bitter, but she heard the anger in her tone as clearly as Lykos did. "It is my master's right to do that, but it is a difficult burden."

"I would think so," Lykos said without too much obvious sympathy. "I was told by Himic that you are trying to get sufficient money to purchase the freedom of your father and his wives and children."

"Yes. Chimbue Barantosz, who was my first master, has agreed to keep the price for their freedom at a fixed rate for another three and a half years. After that, we will see." She picked up a pitchfork. "I must get the bedding up. If you do not mind?"

"Go ahead." He stood back while she got a shovel and went into Shirdas' stall. "Your father is still a slave of Barantosz's, then?"

"Yes. He's Armenian, living in Cappadocia. Barantosz's father bought him from an Armenian noble when my father was younger than I am now. Barantosz has kept the family together to help him with the horses he raises." She had shoveled most of the used straw out the door of the stall and was now forking down fresh bedding from the loft above. "He trained me, my father, as his father had trained him. My father said that our family has done stunt riding for more than five generations."

"A proud heritage," Lykos agreed. "You have developed more skills, or so Himic informs me."

"Himic has been very good to me, teaching me all manner of skills and new stunts. He has shown me how to perform so that the audience will like what I do better, and he has helped me do what I do better." She was almost finished with the bedding when she stopped. "There is something strange in this straw. It smells peculiar."

Lykos stepped closer. "What is it like?"

"I don't know." She lifted the pitchfork closer to her face, sniffing. "It's sort of sweet—sticky smelling." She sniffed again and felt a queasy sensation go through her.

"You had better toss that straw out and let my men inspect the loft. It could be that this is another attempt to interfere." He said this calmly. "I have seen similar things done in Ancona and Roma. My men know what to look for." He did not wait to see if Tishtry followed his instructions, but hurried to the stable entrance. "Marcos, Cyral, Demobri, into the loft. Check the straw for tampering."

Tishtry had cleaned out two more of the stalls, adding no new bedding, when Lykos came to her. "Someone has made a mixture of syrup of poppies and syrup of hemp and put it on the straw. At the least, it would have made your horses drowsy and inactive. At the most, they would have collapsed in a stupor."

"What . . . how?" She was filled with a baffled rage. "How dare they try to harm my team?"

Lykos chuckled grimly. "Whoever it was, they will not try again. You have my word on it." His blue eyes met her dark ones. "Be complimented, girl. Someone out there is afraid you're going to win."

CHAPTER
XVII

At the beginning of the Games, there was a parade. Calpurnius and Valericus, as editoris, rode in the first chariot, this one a huge vehicle, drawn by twelve matched Egyptian horses the color of coral. There were slaves on the chariot who were dressed like Grecian gods and goddesses, all wearing sheer garments of fine Coan linen; they threw flowers and fragrant herbs over the arena and waved happily to the crowd.

Behind this first chariot came a troupe of musicians, playing their instruments as loudly as possible. Five litui bleated beside five tibiae. Then came a rank of men blowing their corni, each cornum held circling his arm and projecting from behind over his shoulder and head. Last came players of the sistrum and cymbals, making their rackets to a heavy beat.

Immediately after them, Tishtry and Dionysos rode in their chariots, the teams held firmly by their aurigatores, who walked beside the horses, handling the traces so that the horses could not bolt.

"Be careful, girl," Dionysos threatened her, waving blithely at the crowd. "I'm not going to let you win."

"You have nothing to say about what I do," Tishtry answered, and looked down at Himic. "Neronis is trying to get the bit in his teeth. Be careful."

After these two there were groups of fighters—gladiators, secutores, retiarii, essedarii, and the rest—and then some of the bestiarii with their trained animals whose performance would conclude the first day of the Games. The crowd hailed them all with noisy enthusiasm.

They went around the arena twice, then exited through the Gates of Life, each group gathering in the area set aside for it. Near the stables, the physician set up his bench and sorted out his unguents and splints and knives, preparing for the injuries he would treat throughout the day.

Calpurnius came through the crowd, pushing the arena slaves aside. "Tishtry!" he called as he neared her. "I must have a word with you!"

Tishtry, who was starting her last inspection of her chariot, turned toward him. "Yes, my master? What is it?"

He grabbed her by the arm and pulled her near the Gates of Life. In a furious whisper, he said, "Lose!"

Her face went white. "What are you saying?" She tried to laugh and discovered that she could not. "You . . . it isn't amusing, my master."

"It's not meant to be," he hissed. "I order you to

194

lose." He glared at her. "I've bet against you. Do you understand me? If you want to be sold at an advantage, you will go out there and lose. I will have the profit from your sale and the money from the bets. Do you understand!" He pushed at her shoulder. "Do as I tell you." With that, he spun away from her and was lost among the men gathered at the Gates of Life.

Tishtry stared blankly ahead, trying to make sense of what he had told her to do. It seemed impossible that, after so much preparation, he would actually tell her she was not to win. Then she thought that he had bet against her, and that made her angry in a way she had never felt before. "How *dare* he?" she whispered, glaring at the Gates of Life.

Himic came and touched her shoulder. "Tishtry?"

"What?" She rounded on him furiously. "Calpurnius has already spoken to me."

"When?" Himic was clearly puzzled by this outburst. "What is the matter, girl? You can't be getting nervous now, can you?" He patted her arm tentatively. "If you're troubled, tell me about it and I will do what I can for you." The tone of his voice was sincere, and Tishtry wondered if Himic knew of their master's betrayal. "The team is ready, and the contest is about to begin."

"Did you place any bets?" she demanded of him. "Did you?"

"Yes," he admitted.

"How did you bet?" She turned her eyes up at him. "Well?"

"What kind of question is that?" Himic asked her, annoyance changing his attitude to a more critical one.

"Did you bet on me to win or lose?" she asked harshly.

Himic laughed. "What's wrong with you, girl? We both know you'll win."

"Truly?" she said, still unconvinced of his innocence.

"Naturally. I've seen you and Dionysos in the arena, and I've seen you practice. You're the better horseman, and you're the better performer. Of course you're going to win. All you have to do is concentrate." He frowned. "Have you been offered a bribe not to win?"

"Not a bribe, an order," she said. "Calpurnius said I am to lose. And Himic, I don't want to!" Tears came to her eyes without warning. "I want to win. I want to show that I can win!"

"You must have misunderstood," Himic said, staring at her. "Calpurnius would not issue such an order. He could not." He held up his hand as Lykos came toward them. "You should not say such things, girl."

"*I* shouldn't?" she burst out. "It is Calpurnius who should not say such things. Calpurnius is the one who has—" She stopped abruptly and looked away from Himic.

Lykos saw that something was troubling Tishtry, for he regarded her seriously. "Are you worried about the race?" He held out his hand, which contained a small knife. "In the Circus Maximus in Roma, all charioteers carry these. They are to cut yourself free of the traces if there is an accident, so that you will not get dragged or kicked."

Tishtry took the knife. "Where did you get this?"

He hesitated before he answered. "Your master gave it to me."

"My master?" Tishtry repeated, making no effort to

conceal her amazement. "Why would he do this? Calpurnius just told me to lose and now he sends me a knife. What does he expect me to do, slit my own throat?"

"Did Calpurnius give you orders? When?" Lykos asked sharply.

"Just now." She scowled. "He said I was to lose. He is my master, and he wants me to lose!" She smashed her fist onto her thigh.

"But he is not your master," Lykos said. "When I saw Calpurnius approach you, I thought it was to tell you . . ." He glanced at Himic. "Calpurnius sold you this morning. Your new owner is a foreigner named Franciscus." He paused. "You need not obey Calpurnius. In anything." This last afterthought was accompanied by a tight, grim smile. "You need only do the best you can."

"Calpurnius already sold me!" Tishtry exclaimed, staring at Himic. "Do you know anything about this?"

Himic shook his head, stunned at what he had heard.

"So you have no reason to do as Calpurnius told you," Lykos said. "Go on. Your quadriga is waiting. Win if you can." He made a gesture of encouragement, then stepped back. "I will see you when it is over."

Though she was still caught up in her surprise, Tishtry was able to nod to Lykos. "Afterward," she said, starting toward her chariot with a new sense of purpose.

The Gates of Life swung open and the audience roared as energetically as lions. Tishtry drew up her team at the alba linea, holding her restless horses as Dionysos thundered up in his ten-horse rig. She nodded to him and did not mind that he ignored her.

In the editoris' box, Valericus leaned forward, to drop the white handkerchief to start the race.

"These are the rules!" the Master of the Games bawled out, trying to be heard over the voices of the crowd. "You will have seven circuits of the arena, each to be completed with one trick or stunt during the circuit. If at any time a lap is completed without a trick, that lap will be disallowed in the total of the race. At the end of seven laps, the first chariot to be drawn up at the editoris' box will be declared the winner, providing the correct number of stunts has been completed!" The man, purple in the face from his effort, stepped back to stand beside Valericus.

"Be on guard, girl!" Dionysos hissed as the handkerchief fell and the race began.

Dionysos took the lead at first, cutting ahead of Tishtry and using his team to block her from advancing. As he drove, he climbed up on the inside of his chariot and stood on the top of the vehicle, balancing as the team plunged ahead.

Nothing daunted, Tishtry launched herself onto her team's backs, somersaulting from one horse to the other, then backflipping into the chariot before urging them to pass Dionysos' team on the outside. It was a very risky move and one she was apprehensive of making, but she did not want Dionysos to hold the lead one moment longer than necessary. As she brought her team close to his, he countered the move by signaling his horses to rush to the side, throwing Tishtry's horses off their stride.

There was a shout from the crowd as Dionysos drew his team up onto their hind legs and kept them advancing, their front hooves in the air. Dionysos grinned at the reception of his trick, and he made a rude sign to Tishtry, which she answered with one that was even ruder.

On the second lap, Tishtry once again got onto the backs of her team, this time standing on her hands while her team tried once again to get past Dionysos' ten horses. From her place on Amath's back, Tishtry shouted instructions to her horses, relying on her voice instead of the signals of her reins. She could feel Amath almost break stride as Dionysos once again urged his horses in the direction of her chariot.

The crowd was growing even noisier as the competition went into the third lap. Tishtry wondered what stunt Dionysos had done on the second lap, and thought that the rearing was not as much of a stunt as it ought to be. She wondered if she should protest that stunt later, when the final decision was made about who won the race. She vaulted onto Immit's back and got to her feet on the dun mare's rump, bracing herself as the horses rounded the end of the arena and began the third lap. Now she was prepared to go under the necks of her team. It was more difficult without the three outer horses yoked together, but she had practiced it enough that she was certain she would be able to do it safely.

Dionysos brought his team up close to hers just as Tishtry started to swing under Shirdas' neck. He signaled his lead rank of horses to veer toward her, knocking into Amath, so that the bay staggered and lurched against Neronis.

Shirdas faltered in his canter and Tishtry was almost flung free of her horse. She clung to his neck, making no attempt to move while Shirdas steadied himself, and the other three horses resumed their steady canter. When she was certain that it was safe to move, she swung under Shirdas' neck, reaching for the base of Immit's mane.

Once again Dionysos slammed his team into Tishtry's, and this time she was so badly jarred that her shoulder wrenched and pain shot along her arm and almost made her let go of the mane she held. She gripped convulsively, for the first time afraid that she might fall and be trampled. With an agonizing effort, she pulled herself onto Immit's back, gathering her strength before she got to her feet. Her left arm ached terribly and she was not sure she could complete her next swing under Neronis' neck and onto Amath's back.

Now Dionysos was dropping back, trying to find a way to hook the wheel of his chariot with the wheel of hers. It was a tricky maneuver, and one that was very dangerous, for it could lead to both vehicles being wrecked. The size of his team got in his way, and he was not able to get near enough to bring the two wheels close together.

Tishtry took advantage of this and urged her team into the lead, then swung under Neronis' neck and onto Amath's back before Dionysos could slam her horses again. She knew that she would not be able to hold on through another such violent collision. As she rose to her feet on Amath's back, she could feel the big bay limping a bit. She looked to his head, and saw him duck, slightly and regularly, as he ran. One of the impacts the bay had taken had injured him somehow, and

Tishtry would not know how seriously until this hideous race was finished.

Dionysos was trying to pass her on the outside again, holding his team as close to hers as he could without another impact. Amath ran with his ears back, no longer matching the stride of the other horses in Tishtry's team. There were flecks of foam on his dark coat, and he was already panting heavily. Tishtry could feel the strain through his muscles, quickly leaped into the air, somersaulting onto Neronis' back to give Amath a chance to recover. She thought of the tricks she wanted to do and worked out ways to do them without using Amath again. The pressure of Dionysos' team was making her own horses run faster, no longer coordinated in their strides. Tishtry vaulted back into the chariot, and as she did, she heard an ominous crack from one of the wheels, and the chariot wobbled under her.

The crowd shouted and screamed, and the noise frightened her horses in a way they had not been scared before. Immit strained her neck out, striving to get the bit in her teeth.

With a quick move, Dionysos swung his team into Tishtry's one more time, and this effort was more damaging. The outside wheel broke three of its spokes and flailed on the axle, no longer secure. Over the sound of the crowd, Tishtry could hear Dionysos laugh.

Tishtry abandoned her earlier plans and got back onto her horses' backs, doing a dance step from Shirdas to Immit to Neronis, but leaving Amath to run without hindrance. She did the splits across the three horses' backs, then leaned down between the big animals and started to cut her team free of the chariot, which was floundering behind them. The first harness lines parted, and she got over onto the next horse, trying to reach the broad leather straps as she felt Shirdas and Immit surge ahead. She reached her traces and held the two free-running horses in with the two still attached to the chariot. There were two more laps to go, and she could sense that Dionysos had not finished with her yet. Her hands were slick with sweat as she grabbed the harness line between Neronis and Amath.

Suddenly Dionysos cut in front of her, and this time Amath gave a screaming whinny and stumbled, falling as Tishtry cut the line holding him to the chariot. He fell heavily to his side, the chariot coming to rest against his flank as his hooves pawed at the air.

Tishtry was distressed, and worry for her horse almost made her draw in her team, but she was too close to winning now. She gathered up the traces and stood on Immit's rump, letting Neronis and Shirdas run a bit ahead of the dun mare. It was something she had only done with her team on the lunge, and she hoped that they would not be too confused to complete the maneuver.

Ahead of her, Dionysos was taking his team into the curve. His grin was as broad as she had ever seen it, and she wanted to throw herself into his chariot and battle him there like a gladiator.

Amath had got to his feet and pulled himself to the side of the arena. He put no weight at all on his off rear leg, and as Tishtry approached him, she could see that the leg was broken. Her heart went cold inside her.

One more circuit, one last trick, Tishtry told herself

as she tried to ignore her fatally injured horse. Then she would win, and could tend to her team. The desire to defy Calpurnius had left her with the sight of Amath leaning against the wall, his head down, resignation in every line of his body.

Dionysos swung in front of Tishtry, signaling his horses to fan out so that she could not pass on either side of him. He was looking back over his shoulder, making a sign of victory, when his team ran into her overturned chariot.

The screams and neighing of his team were drowned in the bellow from the crowd. Dionysos was catapulted out of his chariot and fell among the thrashing hooves of his animals.

Tishtry pulled her three horses into a walk, and still standing on Immit's back, she made her team walk around the wreck in single file, then brought them into their standard abreast formation as she drew them up in front of the editoris' box.

At either end of the arena, the Gates of Life and the Gates of Death were flung open, and arena slaves rushed onto the sands, hurrying to aid Dionysos and his ten matched horses, all caught in a horrible tangle thirty paces behind Tishtry.

From her place on Immit's rump, Tishtry saluted the two Romans in the editoris' box, and without waiting for their response, she wheeled her three horses and rode them out through the Gates of Life.

XVIII

Himic shook his head as he came out of Amath's stall. "There is nothing more we can do for him. One of the grooms will take care of . . ." He did not finish.

Tishtry nodded. She went to the door of the stall and reached through to pet the bay's soft nose. "I'm sorry, old boy," she whispered, feeling tears on her face. "I'm sorry."

"The Master of the Games has impounded the chariot, to examine it for possible signs of tampering," Himic said behind her. "There isn't much left of it, not with what Dionysos' team did to it, but the law requires that the thing be inspected."

"Fine," she said, still touching Amath in affection and grief. "That wheel did not break of its own accord."

"Probably not," Himic agreed. "Come, girl. Leave Amath to the grooms now. He's suffering."

"I know." She forced herself to turn away, to take

her mind off Amath. "What about Dionysos. How badly is he hurt?"

"The physician hasn't finished with him yet, but he has broken his arm and a few ribs for sure. There are cuts on his face; when he heals he won't be quite as pretty as he was before, but better that than crippled, I suppose." Himic deliberately led her out of the stables. "He is claiming that there was sabotage of the contest, and Valericus has said that he will do what he can to find out if anyone attempted to harm his team."

Tishtry had fallen into step beside her aurigatore. "Himic, have you been bought, as well?"

Himic stopped. "No. I am to stay with Calpurnius, to train the next promising youngster my master finds." He looked down at Tishtry. "Whoever it is, he won't be as good as you are, girl. You're the kind a man like me gets to train once in a lifetime."

Her throat, already tight, now felt as if it had closed entirely. "Oh, Himic, what is going to become of me?"

He took her by her shoulders and did his best to smile. "Why, you will go on to Ancona—that's all arranged—and from there to Roma, where you will perform in the Circus Maximus, just as you have always wanted to do. You will have a dozen horses of your own, and half a dozen chariots, and by the time you retire and buy your freedom, you will have money enough to own Calpurnius three times over. You'll see."

"I'll buy you then," she said, her voice quivering as she strove to keep from crying in earnest.

"Oh, don't worry about me. In a few years, I will be able to retire to the back of the stables, and all I will have to do is tend the horses and see that the mares drop healthy foals. Perhaps my master will provide me with a woman, and we'll drop a few children of our own."

Tishtry knew that she was supposed to laugh at this, but she could only shake her head. "I will miss you, Himic. Without your help, I would never have done . . . any of this."

"Of course you would have," he said, thrusting her away from him. "It would have taken a little longer, perhaps, but nothing could have stopped you once you set your heart on your goal." Impulsively, he gave her a hug, then he growled, "Lykos is waiting for you, over by the Gates of Life. He needs to make arrangements for the shipment of your team."

At this mention of her horses, Tishtry looked back over her shoulder toward the stables. "Amath . . ."

"Never mind Amath. Leave him be." Himic sighed. "You have other horses to look after."

"I'll have to inspect their legs and feet once they have been cooled," she said, her habits reasserting themselves.

"This time the authorities of the amphitheater will tend to that. More of their investigation into that accident." He pointed to where Lykos stood. "Go on. Your new master will want you to be prepared to depart soon."

"Must I?" she wailed. It had all been too much—the contest, the injury to Amath, the accident that had hurt Dionysos—and to have to leave now made her feel that she was losing everything.

"Lykos says your new master is kind. Don't keep him waiting too long," Himic told her gruffly, then turned on his heel and walked away from her, not looking back as he went.

Tishtry watched him go, and for once in her life made no attempt to be brave. She wept bitterly, standing by herself in a cocoon of misery while other arena performers milled around her, paying very little attention to her.

Finally she wiped the tears from her face with her grubby hands and went to speak to Lykos.

"The Master of the Games has ordered Calpurnius fined," Lykos told Tishtry three days later while he supervised the loading of her gear. "In telling you to lose, he broke the law against suborning slaves. The fact that he told you to lose is bad enough, but that he had already sold you and did not inform you of the fact is very bad indeed. His slaves have been banned from the amphitheater for a period of a year, and he is not allowed to sponsor any more Games for a period of five years." He signaled to one of the slaves who had accompanied him to pick up her chest of belongings. "Take that to the ship and see that it is safely stowed."

Tishtry sat on a bench near the window of the tavern where Lykos had secured her a room. "What is it like in Ancona?"

"Well, the amphitheater is much larger than this one. Ancona seats almost twice as many people as the amphitheater here in Salonae, and neither is anywhere near the size of the Circus Maximus. Franciscus has said that he wishes you to work in Ancona until you are comfortable with the larger arena, and then he will arrange for you to go to Roma." He came and patted

207

her on the shoulder. "You will have a year to train your new team. Franciscus has sent word that you will have your pick of twenty horses. He is giving you six of them to begin with." Both of them knew that this was remarkably generous. "He has also set aside a portion of your winnings for you."

"What?" Tishtry looked up at Lykos. "You mean the horses are not all?"

"Apparently not," Lykos said, smiling a bit, though with features as austere as his, it was hard to tell if his expression was intended to be a smile.

"So I go from a greedy master to a mad one." She sighed. "And in time, who knows what sort of man will buy me?"

"That is for the future, and the gods will decide," Lykos said with surprising gentleness. "Come, girl. It is time to leave."

Tishtry got to her feet. "Very well. Show me where I am to go." She thought of her arrival in Salonae, and the confusion she had found when she had got off the ship. She had grown used to the size and chaos of the place and knew that she would miss it.

"There is a Greek merchantman waiting for us. Your horses are already aboard, and aside from you and me, it is ready to sail." Lykos gestured toward the door.

"Himic didn't say good-bye," Tishtry mused as she followed Lykos out of the tavern.

"He is Calpurnius' slave; he would not be permitted to do such a thing," Lykos remarked as he led the way toward the waterfront.

"Still," she murmured, then fell silent as she turned her back on Salonae.

Her new collar was made of amber and silver, and was finer and lighter than any she had worn before. Her owner's name was embossed on it, and her own as well. Tishtry had almost got used to it by the time she arrived in Ancona, two days after leaving Salonae.

"There are quarters for arena slaves near the amphitheater," Lykos explained to her as they left the ship. "Space has been reserved for you by your master, and he has arranged for the horses I mentioned to be brought here before the next full moon. That will give you a little time to work with your four horses so that you will be ready to show your master what your team can do already."

Tishtry found it difficult to generate any real interest in performing, for she was still saddened by the loss of Amath, and her shoulder ached whenever she put too much weight on it, or tried to lift anything heavy. "It will take a little time, I think" was all she was willing to say.

Lykos did not remark on her attitude, but merely told her to go with his men and they would take her to her quarters. "There are baths adjoining the slaves' quarters, and they will tend to you. Be sure you mention your injuries so that the masseur will know what to do for you."

Tishtry was tempted to stay with her horses and to delay going to her new quarters, but she could read determination in Lykos' face and decided she would not argue with him. "All right. But I will want to see my team after they are taken to their stalls."

"Of course. One of the grooms will show you the

way. You have only to ask." Lykos paused, then added this one precaution. "There are more than two hundred horses stabled here at the amphitheater. Let the grooms guide you."

"All right," she said, too downcast to be impressed by the number of horses Lykos had mentioned. As she followed Lykos' man through the crowded streets, she noticed the lack of bigae and carts and eventually she asked about it.

"There are rules here, as in Roma. On days when the swine market is open, only foot traffic, sedan chairs, and single-horse vehicles are allowed within the city walls from an hour after sunrise to an hour before sunset. Otherwise no one would be able to move on these streets." He pointed out a thermopolium where sausages were being heated on a grill and huge vats of wine sunk into the counter open to the street attracted customers. "If you want a quick meal, these are the places to go. Some of them serve grilled fish as well as sausages."

Tishtry nodded, wanting to appear familiar with the city. The aroma of the food blended with the smell of livestock from the nearby market and the general crush of humanity around her. "The people here smell . . . different."

"Proper Romans bathe often and have the grace to use fresh scent. The clothes are washed to keep them fresh. We're not like some of the barbarians of the Empire who . . ." He stopped, remembering that Tishtry was an Armenian from Cappadocia. "Of course, many of the client countries have taken to our ways."

"Of course," Tishtry said politely, though she wanted to kick him for his attitude.

But later, when she had seen her quarters—two rooms and a large closet for storing her tack and her clothing—she went along to the baths, going first to the tepidarium for mild exercise and a refreshing dip in cool water. Then she went into the caldarium, to sit in the hot, steamy darkness in a small pool of hot water. She felt the tightness in her shoulder begin to ease and her fatigue let go of her. After that, she went briefly to the frigidarium to splash herself with cold water before going to the masseur, who spread sweet-smelling oil over her, then set to work kneading all her muscles, giving special attention to her shoulder and back.

"I have an ointment of rose oil, white cedar, and thyme that will help your shoulder," the masseur said when he was almost through with his work. "If you rub it into your shoulder in the morning and after exercise, it will ease the strain."

"Thanks," Tishtry murmured, feeling so relaxed now that she feared they would have to pour her into a cask to get her back to her quarters. "I'll do it."

"Your master has sent word that you're to have massage twice a week as part of your training routine," the masseur went on. "He orders that for all his arena slaves."

"Does he have many?" Tishtry asked, touched with interest now.

"I have heard that he has quite a few; no fighters, just performers. It's easier for foreigners to have performers." The masseur finished up with her hands and

211

feet, then dismissed her, telling her to move slowly for an hour or so.

That night Tishtry slept deeply, and by morning she felt restored as she rubbed ointment into her shoulder and went out to inspect her team. She had them on the lunge in one of the smaller practice rings—the amphitheater at Salonae had had just one, but Ancona had four—when a stranger approached her, watching from the fence while she worked.

He was very still, this stranger; he made no impatient movement, no distracting gestures, until Tishtry released her team to let them run on their own for a bit, then he came through the gate into the ring, walking up to Tishtry as he offered a greeting.

She returned it, shading her eyes to study him. "You are?"

"Franciscus," he said. He was taller than most Romans, dressed in a short black Persian tunica and black leggings worn with red Scythian boots. His hair and eyes were dark.

"My master?" she said, impressed in spite of herself.

"Yes." His shadow fell across her. "You are quite expert with your horses," he said.

"Does that surprise you?" she asked, a bit surprised herself.

"No." He reached for a pouch that hung at his belt. "You are entitled to five percent of your winnings. That is the custom among Romans." The pouch was a large one, filled with coins. "They are all gold and silver; no copper. There are forty-one aurei and sixty-eight denarii."

Her eyes widened at the sum. "So much?" With what

she had saved already, she had more than enough to buy her family's freedom at last.

"Some of it should have been given you before; Calpurnius withheld part of your winnings for his own use. The magistrates at Salonae released the money to me when they recorded your sale. Lykos brought the documents to me when he returned here with you." He looked down at her as she took the pouch. "Is there anything you require?"

"I . . ." Now that it was possible to free her family, she did not know how to go about it. "My family . . . I want . . ."

"Lykos told me," he said with a faint, kind smile. "You wish to buy their freedom. They are owned by a Cappadocian horse breeder—"

"Chimbue Barantosz," she supplied, nodding.

"—who has agreed to hold the price level for you." He paused. "Would you like to arrange the transfer of funds? I own several merchant ships that trade in Cappadocia. It would not be difficult to send a messenger to Barantosz."

Tishtry's eyes lit up. "Oh, would you?"

Franciscus' smile lasted longer this time. "It would be my honor."

Although it was improper to behave this way in front of her master, Tishtry leaped into the air with a whoop. It was real! She had done it! Her family would be free! She would perform in Roma!

Her horses shied at her outburst, and she recalled herself and made the effort to be more circumspect. "I am . . . grateful."

"I think I like the yell better," Franciscus said ruefully. Then he put his small, well-shaped hand on her shoulder. "Come. There are horses you must inspect and two or three quadrigae to try out. Then we will arrange for the messenger to Barantosz."

Tishtry was so giddy with her sudden happiness that she skipped instead of walking, and this time she made no apology. As they reached the gate, she looked up at her master. "I have a great many plans," she said, trying to anticipate his reaction.

"Good: so have I." He held the gate open and they went through together.

GLOSSARY

ALBA LINEA: literally, white line. The starting point of a chariot race.

AMPHITHEATER: the actual structure where the Great Games were held. The Circus Maximus in Rome seated over 50,000 spectators.

ARENA (pl. ARENAE): literally, sand. The performing area of the Roman amphitheater.

AUREUS (pl. AUREI): a gold coin, worth about twenty-five denarii or, in modern terms, between $35.00 and $50.00.

AURIGATORE: a slave who took care of a chariot, the harness, bridles, yokes, and other gear, though not the horses.

BESTIARII: a performing slave working specifically with animals. Racing charioteers were not bestiarii; stunt riders were.

BIGA (pl. BIGAE): a small chariot pulled by two horses.

BIREME: a ship with two ranks of oars, one above the other.

CALDARIUM: a hot bath, usually taken in a small, waist-

215

deep tub large enough to accommodate four to ten persons.

CALIGULA (pl. CALIGULAE): the type of sandals worn by soldiers.

CARACALLA: the long military cape worn by officers and Legion troops.

DALMATICA (pl. DALMATICAE): a caftanlike garment, the most popular Roman dress. Used for business, social, and casual entertaining events, but not formal occasions.

DENARIUS (pl. DENARII): a silver coin worth about $1.40 to $2.00 in modern terms.

DISEASE OF THE CRAB: skin cancer (cancer is the Latin word for crab).

EDITOR (pl. EDITORIS): the sponsor and patron of the Great Games, usually a noble or someone with political ambitions.

ESSEDARIUS (pl. ESSEDARII): a performing slave, often used in arena combat. The essedarius drove a high-fronted chariot and disabled opponents with a lasso.

FIVE-GAITED (five-paced): the "natural" gaits of horses are walk, trot, canter, and gallop. There are a number of "artificial" gaits, including racking, pacing, and the advanced steps of formal dressage.

FOUNDER: to become injured or inflamed, as the hooves of a horse, causing lameness or similar disability.

FREEDMAN: a slave who has received a grant of manumission, thereby gaining freedom.

FREEMAN: any person born free of free or freed parents.

FRIGIDARIUM: a cold bath, usually shallow, often located in the darkest part of a Roman bath complex. A frigidarium usually held no more than six people at a time.

GATES OF DEATH: usually at the opposite end of the amphitheater from the Gates of Life. Those humans and animals that did not survive in the arena were taken out through the Gates of Death.

GATES OF LIFE: the gates through which all arena slaves entered the arena except during certain aquatic events. If the slaves and their animals survived in the arena, they left through these gates as well.

GREAT GAMES: any arrangement of amphitheater performances, usually including chariot races, various combats and hunts, and trained animal acts. In Latin, Ludi Maximi.

LIQUAMEN: a sauce used in Roman cooking made of fermented fish. About as popular as mustard and catsup, and used as frequently.

LITUUS (pl. LITUI): literally, a staff of office. In this case, a brass instrument, long and thin, with a narrow bell curved back toward the player.

LUNGE: sometimes called a long line; a single long rein used by the equestrian to work with the horse while not riding it. The equestrian stands in an exercise area and works the horse on the lunge in a circle.

MAJORDOMO: literally, in charge of the house. A slave responsible for a household, something like a butler.

MASTER OF THE BESTIARII: a slave or freeman responsible for the securing and public appearance of animal acts at a specific amphitheater.

META (pl. METAE): conical fenders located at either end of the spina.

QUADRIGA (pl. QUADRIGAE): a chariot pulled by four horses. Racing quadrigae were lighter and smaller than road-use quadrigae and required more skill to drive.

RETIARIUS (pl. RETIARII): an arena combat slave fighting with a net and long-handled trident, usually against secutores.

SECUTOR (pl. SECUTORES): an arena combat slave fighting with a round shield, metal helmet, metal-studded leather shoulder armor, and a short sword, usually against retiarii.

SPINA: literally, spine. The dividing wall down the middle of the arena, ranging from four to twenty feet in height, depending on the size of the amphitheater and what the amphitheater was equipped to do.

TEPIDARIUM: a cool bath, often very large, like a swimming pool. The tepidarium usually adjoined a gymnasium and was a place to socialize as well as take exercise, swim, and have a massage.

THERMOPOLIUM: a fast-food grill, usually a street-side business, specializing in hot foods and wine. A thermopolium offered limited seating, and the quality of the food served ranged from terrible to marvelous.

TIBIA (pl. TIBIAE): literally, a shinbone. A Roman musical instrument, with a double-reed mouthpiece like the modern oboe and with four to eight finger holes.

TUNICA (pl. TUNICAE): a standard garment in Roman dress. It was knee length, cut in an A shape, usually but not always without sleeves. Horsemen wore it with leggings. In winter several woolen tunicae were worn; in summer a single tunica of linen, cotton, or silk replaced them. The standard garment for children, informal social occasions, sports, and around-the-house wear.

VENATION: an arena hunt. Usually specific animals would be hunted by specific hunters, such as wild boar hunted by dwarves, or ostriches being hunted by wolf hounds.